I0607946

BEACH MAGIC

THE ELEMENTAL KEYS BOOK 4

LYNNE CANTWELL

hearth/myth

Copyright 2020 by Lynne Cantwell

Cover designed in GIMP

a hearth/myth book

TABLE OF CONTENTS

HOW WE GOT HERE

So here we are again, the four of us. At least we're not waiting for a plane this time. And for once, we may have bought ourselves some breathing room.

First things first, though. The stars of our story are four half-human Elementals: Gail Oleander, the Airy half-sylph; Rufus McKay, the Fiery half-salamander (the magic kind, not the lives-under-your-porch kind); Collum Barth, the Earthy half-gnome; and me, Raney Meadows, a Watery half-undine and out-of-work actress. We met in Harpers Ferry, West Virginia, where the spirit of the Shenandoah River put Collum's brother's dead body where I would find it. Then Collum found me, we met the others, a guy named Cassius swept us away to a crucible where we exchanged Elemental juices, and hey presto, we were a team – although not the well-oiled machine we ought to be, considering we all have a part of each other within us now.

We even have superhero names. I'm the Torrent. And finally – finally! – we have team t-shirts! I bought them at the outfitter store in Denver where we geared up this morning. They are really cool, featuring all kinds of awesome qualities that we stand for, like courage and compassion and gratitude and fun.

Well, some of our adventures have been more fun than others.

Actually, most of what we've been through hasn't been much fun at all.

See, Collum's brother Conor was killed because he knew too much. My father, Damien Jones – who's a narcissistic sociopath, among his other endearing traits – had played a long con on a guy who owned a construction company in West Virginia. Damien, or rather the ancient evil thing riding him, made the guy a state representative in exchange for helping him lop off the top of a mountain to get to a big coal seam underneath. Unfortunately for my father, Collum's family had stationed a land wight in the way.

But Damien still got away with a magical Key that fits a door behind which is a Tool of Ultimate Destruction. We assumed, when he headed to Ireland, that that was where the door was. Haha no – we've since learned that there are four Keys, one for each Element. The Water Key was what he got in West Virginia. The Earth Key was in Ireland, in County Kilkenny, and Collum's father was in charge of guarding it. Which should have made it easy for us to protect, right?

Once Damien got to Ireland, he tried to pull the same con he had in West Virginia. He promised the moon and the stars to the operator of a peat processing plant in County Kilkenny in exchange for helping him find the Earth Key.

The four of us managed to dodge Damien and the thing riding him – it's a demon, by the way, named Surgat, which means "He Who Opens All Locks" – as well as the golems brought to life by the demon, in order to get the Key to safekeeping. Except the new hidey hole didn't turn out to be as safe as we thought it was. Surgat snatched the Earth Key out from under our noses.

So off we went to Hawaii to try to grab the Fire Key before Damien could figure out where it was. It almost worked, too, except we ran into my asshole of an ex-boyfriend on the Big Island and somehow, once *he* knew I was there, Damien knew right where to find us. We retrieved the Key anyway, with the help of the ancestral Hawaiian guardian spirits – in particular a gecko named Moe with an amazing morphing ability – but the box the Fire Key was in was super-hot and Gail bobbled it and, well, now Surgat has three of the four Keys.

Gail's been beating herself up over that. We're now in Colorado, at the base of Mt. Elbert, and she is not about to let anything get between her and the Air Key – not Damien, not Surgat, and for sure not the snitty sylph who's guarding the Key.

I'm not sure why the sylph has been so cranky. I mean, I know she's in contact with the fae, and the fae are mad at us because I didn't fall for their stupid deal in Ireland. Like I was born yesterday or something.

The Tuatha de Danaan, however, are on our side. So are the world's Water spirits, and the Hawaiian aumakua, and a land wight named Cloch. That is, I *think* the wight is with us. Last I knew, he was still pretty sore at Collum and his family for sequestering him next to that coal seam in West Virginia.

Anyway, we're here now, with a sylph who was mad at us up until about ten minutes ago, when Collum and Rufus sequestered my father and the demon. Now this same sylph is supposed to lead us on a hike up one of the highest mountains in North America. I know it sounds chancy, but everybody's wearing their team t-shirt. We're going to win this round, I just know it!

CHAPTER 1 – TUESDAY'S LOOKING (FOURTEEN THOUSAND FEET) UP

Eyes on the prize, I told myself, even as I heard the siren song of the spirits of Colorado's Twin Lakes behind me. Those spirits had already sucked me in once today, and I didn't need any further distractions. For ahead of the rental SUV I was driving fluttered a sylph named Anemone, the guardian of the Air Key. She was supposed to be guiding us to the Mt. Elbert trailhead, but I didn't trust her.

Oh right, I did say "we." That would be my three Elemental teammates and me. In the back seat was Rufus McKay, a.k.a. the Madman. My favorite gnome, Collum Barth, rode shotgun. He's known as the Leprechaun. Our resident Air Elemental, Gail Oleander, was ahead of us, keeping an eye on her fellow sylph. Gail didn't trust Anemone, either.

And I'm Raney Meadows, undine. The guys call me the Torrent. I'm confident it has nothing to do with my penchant for bursting into tears at the drop of a hat.

Anemone was mad at us because she thought we were horning in on her job. She knew my father, Damien Jones, was coming to steal the Air Key and she wanted to fight him off herself. Well, technically, it was Surgat, the demon riding my father, who was after the Air Key. The thing already has the other three Elemental Keys and it's after the whole set. Who knew demons were all matchy-matchy?

Honest, though, we were only here to lend a hand. And we proved our worth when Collum and Rufus opened a volcanic rift in the Earth next to the lakes, Gail kicked Damien/Surgat into it, and Collum locked them in. Anemone is still only somewhat chastened, though. I think she suspects us of planning to steal the Air Key ourselves.

I mean, we are. Not gonna lie. But our motives are pure! We're trying to make sure Surgat never gets the full set of Keys, because then he can open a magical door behind which is a Tool of Ultimate Destruction. This tool, whatever it is, can destroy the Earth, or so we've been told. And while humanity hasn't done a bang-up job of protecting the Earth so far, we kind of don't have another planet in reserve if this one goes bye-bye.

I'm told that point has been made again and again in discussions of climate change, yet it hasn't made a dent with some people. Or so I hear. I avoid watching or reading about the news – I'm always worried I'll accidentally see a photo of me that some paparazzi shot from a bad angle or when I wasn't wearing makeup or something. My reputation in Hollywood was bad enough – especially now that the producers of *Story of a Homicide* had bounced me from the show for taking up with this bunch of characters when I was supposed to be hiking the Appalachian Trail.

But I couldn't afford to dwell on my career, or what was left of it, right now. *Eyes on the prize, Raney!*

"Eyes on the road" would have been more helpful. Anemone breezed up a gravel road off the main drag – and when I say *up*, I do mean *up*. I gunned the engine and followed her, the SUV bouncing from rut to pothole.

"The rental agreement didn't prohibit off-roading, did it??" Rufus asked from the back. "Or driving on unpaved roads?"

Collum waved toward the cargo holder between his seat and mine. "The contract's right here, if you want to read it."

"Thanks, but no. Hey, Raney? You'll get more power if you downshift," Rufus said.

I glared at his reflection in the rear-view mirror. "Do you want to do this?"

"Well, actually…"

It was Collum's turn to glare at Rufus. "No," he said. "We don't have time to stop and switch drivers. Raney's doing a fine job. Leave her alone."

"Yeah, leave me alone," I echoed as I swerved to avoid another pothole.

Anemone dodged to the left, in the direction of a "campground this way" sign. Gail made a wide turn to follow her. "They're…" Collum began.

"Thanks," I ground out, and made the turn.

There was no campground host on duty – just a pay station with envelopes and a sign with the campground rules and costs. I took the first available parking spot near the bathrooms. "Okay, everybody out for a potty stop," I said as I opened the door and jumped down.

Rufus laughed. "Did you just say, 'potty stop'?"

"Yes, I did," I said with mock severity. "And the last one out of the bathroom gets to pay for camping." I jogged across the dirt road to the ladies' room.

When I came out, Collum was perusing the map at the pay station. "Did you lose a coin toss?" I asked, sliding my arms around his waist.

He kissed the top of my head. Then he pointed to a spot on the map. "Here we are," he said, "and here's the lower trailhead." His finger moved. Then it moved again. "And here's the upper trailhead. If we start at the lower trailhead, it'll be an eleven-mile-plus hike, round trip. But if we start up here, it'll be only a seven-and-a-half-mile round trip."

"I'm all about the shorter hike," I said as Rufus joined us. "What's the drawback?"

"The road's a little rough to get there." He pointed to a photo that showed mostly boulders.

My eyes widened. "That's a road?"

"Claims to be."

Rufus was vibrating in excitement. "Piece of cake," he said. "I can do it, easy. The car has four-wheel drive, right?"

"I believe so," said Collum.

"I know it does," Rufus said, plowing on. "I saw the switch when it was my turn to drive."

I handed the keys over to him and scanned the parking lot. "Where's Gail? I said. "For that matter, where's Anemone?"

My first question was answered immediately. A breeze whooshed past me and settled into Gail's form. "Gear up," she said shortly. "She's not waiting for us."

"We're leaving *now*?" I said as we walked back to the car. "Isn't it more dangerous to start up in the afternoon? I mean, Flip said…" Flip was the guy who helped us buy all our gear at the outfitter's in Denver. He was very clear on the way big mountains make their own weather. The later in the day it was, the bigger the risk we ran of running into a blizzard before we got to the top.

"We can't wait. Here." Gail handed me a hydration daypack from the back of the SUV.

I put it on, chattering nervously all the while. "But I thought we'd set up the tents and…"

Gail looked as if she were ready to blow. "And what? Take a nap?" She threw a hydration pack at Rufus, who caught it. "What do you think I've been doing for the last ten minutes? Having a lovely cup of tea with Anemone while we caught up on old times?" She grabbed two more packs, shoved one into Collum's arms, and put the other one on. "That bitch is in charge, and she knows we're here to take the Key. She's not planning on making this easy for us."

"Fine," Rufus said, and headed for the driver's door. "We're not planning on playing her game, either. Get in. We're driving to the upper trailhead." He got in the car and grunted in frustration. "My God, Raney, do you *have* to pull the seat so far forward?"

"I do if I want to reach the pedals," I retorted, and got in back. Collum took the front passenger seat again. Gail, still fuming, disappeared in Anemone's direction.

The so-called road to the upper trailhead did not disappoint. It was exactly like the photo at the campground pay station in that it consisted mostly of boulders. I was glad Rufus was driving – if I'd been behind the wheel, I was sure we'd have broken an axle or something.

At last we arrived at the parking lot for the upper trailhead and piled out. Of course there was no sign of Anemone. "Well," Collum growled, "where is she?"

Gail popped in next to me. "Already on the trail and moving fast," she said, and popped out again. I fancied I could still see her glare hanging in the air like a Cheshire cat's smile. Except not. Well, you know.

"I'll go first," Rufus said. "My stride is the longest of the three of us. I'll try to keep sight of everyone," he called over his shoulder.

"Guess that leaves you and me," I said to Collum.

We shared a long look and a quick kiss. "Come on," he said.

That was the last thing any of us said for quite a while. The trail rose steeply to the northwest, robbing us both of breath.

I may be emotional but I'm not stupid; I had actually trained for hiking the Appalachian Trail. But the highest point on the A.T. is Clingman's Dome in Tennessee at 6,643 feet – lower than the elevation we were starting at here by a good four thousand feet. Also, we'd all spent a lot of time at sea level over the past few weeks. The air was a lot thinner here. In short, none of us were in shape for this, and certainly not at this pace.

Flip had tried to warn us. I should have listened better to him. We all should have listened better to him.

After an hour or so of manfully struggling upward, Collum stopped and bent over, gasping. "Just catching my breath," he said between wheezes.

"Hydrate," I ordered, and obediently he sucked from the hose coming from his pack. I did the same. Then I slipped off the daypack and pulled out a couple of Clif bars, handing one to him. He unwrapped it and took two bites. Then he shoved it in his pocket and started up the trail again.

I followed, silently vowing to stay behind him in case he keeled over. I wasn't sure what I could do if it happened – if he tumbled onto me, I wouldn't have had the strength to get him off me. Although I guessed I could force-dissolve and get out from under him that way. Assuming I had the strength myself to do it at that point. I decided adrenaline would be my friend.

Given my thoughts at that moment, I might have been a little light-headed myself. Luckily the elevation gain slowed as we entered an aspen grove. The switchbacks here made the hike even longer, but the golden aspens against the clear, blue sky made the process tolerable. Best of all, we finally had glimpses of Rufus among the trees, and he didn't appear to be that far ahead of us.

Then the trail leveled off and the view opened up. Aspens gave way to a mountain meadow dotted with conifers, and now we had an unobstructed view of Rufus some distance ahead. He stopped and waved to us, then pointed up to where our personal trail marker Gail was phasing in and out as she shadowed Anemone. The altitude didn't seem to affect the sylphs at all. I kind of hated them both right then.

Far ahead of them was the summit of Mt. Elbert – treeless and rocky. Something moved there.

I turned to Collum in alarm. "Did you see that?" And then, seeing him, I was really alarmed. "Collum, are you okay?"

"Just a little light-headed," he said, panting. "I'll be fine."

Yeah, he'd be fine once we got back to the campground. But first, we had to reach the summit, and we still had about three-thousand feet of elevation to gain before we got there.

"Honey, you're coming down with altitude sickness," I said, trying not to panic – or at least trying not to let my panic reach my voice. "You should go back to the car."

He shut his eyes and stood stock-still.

"Collum? What's happening?" I asked, and now I couldn't help it – my fear made my voice shake. "Are you okay? Collum, talk to me!"

He was silent for another moment. I had a quick mental picture of him becoming the mountain, or maybe becoming part of the mountain.

9

As if he were adapting to its environment. As if it had always been his home.

He breathed deeply once, twice, and opened his eyes. "I'm fine," he repeated. He reached into his pocket and finished off the Clif bar in two bites. "Let's go." And he strode away.

I caught up to him. "Did you just cure yourself? You did, didn't you?"

He shrugged. "Mountains are Earth. I just had to tune into this one."

I clutched his arm happily, and he smiled at me. "Did you call me honey just then?" he asked.

"Did I?" I said, with a toss of my head.

He grinned wider.

And then I remembered what I'd been about to say. "Collum, I think there's something waiting…"

I never got the chance to finish. A sudden, howling wind took my breath away. The temperature dropped twenty degrees as clouds crowded out the sun. We'd been told to watch for sudden changes in the weather, but I was pretty sure they weren't usually *this* sudden.

I looked ahead for Gail, but she had vanished. So had Anemone. I hoped Gail had gone after her to make her stop messing with the weather, but there was no way to know for sure.

We struggled against the wind to reach Rufus. We were above the treeline now – there was nowhere to escape the ferocious wind and the bits of ice it drove at us. Our faces stinging, all we could do was plod on.

Chapter 2 – Tuesday, on top of Old Elbie

It seemed as if the three of us had been walking for hours, bent double against the windblown snow, but it was probably only half an hour or so. The snow had begun to pile up, the dirt beneath our feet rapidly turning white.

"This is bullshit!" Rufus suddenly roared above the wind. His eyes turned molten as his body temperature rose. Then he began radiating heat.

The ice pellets stopped striking us; they must have evaporated before they got to us, because we didn't get wet at all. Beneath our feet, the snow melted away as if it had never been there. It didn't even turn the dirt trail to mud.

I heard a tiny shriek of fury, and the wind calmed. The clouds vanished between one blink and the next.

"Thanks, dude," Collum said to Rufus as his eyes returned to their normal muddy brown.

"Don't mention it."

"Well, *I'll* mention it," I said. "Great timing."

"Thanks," Rufus said.

"And I think I know who was responsible," I said.

Gail materialized next to me, holding a tiny, struggling creature aloft between her thumb and forefinger. "I think you do, too, Raney," she said, as the fairy thrashed.

"PUT. ME. DOWN!" the fairy shrieked in her high-pitched whine.

"Not yet," Gail said. "Not until you tell me who put you up to it. Was it Anemone again?"

The creature wailed at an even higher pitch.

I winced and covered my ears, earning inquisitive looks from Rufus and Collum. "You can't hear her?" I said.

"Nope," Collum said. Rufus shrugged.

"Be glad," I said. "Be very glad."

"Stop struggling or I'll put you in a cage!" Gail said.

"YOU WOULDN'T!"

"Try me," said Gail, an evil smile curving her lips. The creature squeaked. Then her movements gradually subsided. "That's better," Gail went on. "Now. Who told you to attack us?"

"TITANIA!" she burst out. "SHE IS MY QUEEN! I HAVE TO DO HER BIDDING!"

"And where is Titania now?" I asked, even though I was pretty sure I knew the answer.

The creature hissed, "She awaits you at the top."

That explained the movement I'd seen at the summit. I nodded and adopted a British accent that I'd picked up as an extra on a BBC drama early in my career. "We shan't keep her waiting, then." I turned to Collum. "If you would be so kind, my lord?"

He bowed — and let me tell you, if you've never seen a gnome in a parka bow from the waist, you're missing out. He then kissed the back of my hand and said, with an Irish accent, "If milady wills it, it shall be so." Then he stepped forward and cut us a gate.

"Dunno why we didn't think of this sooner," Rufus said under his breath.

"My lady," I said to Gail bowing her toward the opening.

"I must decline with thanks, dear undine," she said, her eyes sparkling. "The less this creature sees of the Otherworld, the better off we all shall be. We will meet you at the top." And she breezed away, still holding her captive. The fairy resumed her angry whine, but it cut out with a *pop!* as Gail made like the invisible wind.

I uncovered my ears, making a mental note to thank her later. Then I turned to Collum and Rufus. "You guys seriously couldn't hear that?"

"Nope," said Rufus, and stepped through.

Collum shrugged, then pointed at the gate again. "Go on," he said. "I'll be right behind you."

As I crossed the threshold, I felt again that peculiar sense of nothingness. Then it was over, and I was standing next to Rufus, with Collum just behind. Gail was across from us to our left, still holding the struggling fairy. Anemone had prostrated herself to our right. And in the middle of the misshapen circle were two creatures. One was a woman of normal stature, although a bit on the short side. Her dress was a cross between Victorian finery and Art Nouveau kitsch, and she sported the prettiest pair of wings I'd ever seen. She was presently glowering at everyone in turn, although she appeared to save her harshest vitriol for Anemone. I presumed she was Titania, Queen of the Fae.

The other creature, of course, was Tiger, Collum's dead brother's cat.

"Oh, get up, Anemone," Gail said. "You're a sylph, not a fairy."

"I am too a fairy," Anemone said, her voice somewhat muffled.

"Since when?" Gail barked a laugh. "We are Elementals. We have been here since the Earth began. We are *far* older than the fae. If anything, we outrank her."

"*Silence*, you insolent whelp!" Queen Titania roared.

"I'm no whelp of yours," Gail retorted. She was right, of course – the Elements were created at the same time Earth was. Or maybe Earth was created from the Elements? It's hard to keep track. There's actually a school of philosophy where Elementals spend their days arguing about the nuances, and I couldn't remember which view was currently ascendant.

Anyway, we're definitely not fae. That part Gail had right.

Tiger yawned and began licking her privates. I supposed she wasn't much for philosophical nuance, either.

The queen eyed the cat grimly for a moment, but whatever her knee-jerk reaction would have been, she must have thought better of it. Instead, she transferred her glare to each of us in turn, settling at last on me. "You. Undine."

My guts roiled, but I stood firm and returned her stare, ice queen to ice queen. I inclined my head just so and said, "Very good. Me undine. You fairy queen."

She rolled her eyes. "All right," she said levelly. "Which one of you isn't a smart arse?"

The four of us exchanged questioning looks. Then, as one, we raised our shoulders and smiled.

"Do you want this thing back or not?" Gail asked, wiggling the little fairy in the air.

Titania ignored her. "I shall deal with the gnome," she said, as if issuing a proclamation. "Your name, if you please."

"Collum Barth," he replied. "Of the Kilkenny Barths."

"Ah. A fine family. Always paid their debts, one way or another." She smiled archly. "Your sister, wasn't it?"

Surprised, I turned to Collum. His expression was as hard as if it had been hewn from granite. "Leave her out of this."

"Did you really believe that story your parents told you?" Titania went on. "That she'd died from consumption?"

I was confused for a second, but then I figured it out. *Oh, right. That's what they used to call tuberculosis.*

"She did," Collum said. "I myself heard what the doctor said."

"*Pfft,*" said Titania, dismissing his memory with a wave. "She was taken in payment for services rendered." The queen smiled engagingly. "Would you like to see her?"

"She's bullshitting you," Rufus said, his anger stronger than Collum's.

"And how do you know that, salamander?" said Titania. "The fae have had dealings with your forebears, as well. Why did your cousin Branson take to the drink?"

"Whatever you're insinuating, it isn't true. Alcoholism is a disease," he said.

"That's not what I asked you. I asked you why he began to drink, not why he can't stop." She smiled wickedly. "No response, salamander? Cat got your tongue, perhaps?"

For the record, Tiger informed us, *cats have never gotten anyone's tongue, and we wish people would stop saying that we have.*

Titania threw her a quelling look.

In return, Tiger growled at her. *What's your point, anyway? My people have things to do.*

"My point," Titania said, "is that regardless of which of our tribes came first, each of these *particular* Elementals has a history with the fae." She indicated Anemone, who was still face down in the dirt. "As this one has already acknowledged, and properly so."

"I don't," Gail said.

Titania looked up and tapped her forefinger on her chin. "Let me see… Oh, yes. I remember now. Your great-grandmother asked me to spare her husband's life. *Pleaded* with me. Said she'd do *anything* to save him."

"I don't know anything about it," Gail said stoutly. "They both died before I was born."

"No," said the fairy queen. "Your great-grandmother is with us. We took her when she refused to pay her debt."

"So why is that Gail's problem?" I said.

She turned back to me. "Because, undine, the fae never forget."

"So what do you have on me and mine?" I said. "Let's hear it."

She looked me up and down with disdain. "Nothing," she admitted. "Your mother has proven herself fully capable of creating her own hell."

My anger flared at the insult, but I swallowed it. "Then why…? Oh, I get it. You're mad because I wouldn't make a deal with your minion in Dublin." A fairy had approached me in St Stephen's Green late one night, offering to give me critical information about our mission *for a price.* I'd turned him down.

"That was unfortunate," she said.

"For you, yeah."

"For all of you," she said. "The information I was willing to give you would have made your mission much easier." She side-eyed me coyly. "It's still available, if you want it."

"And the price is the same? No thanks."

She drew herself up as if I'd insulted her. "Fine. That was your last chance, undine. I will see you next in hell." With a shower of glittery fairy dust, she was gone.

Rufus said, "I didn't know the fae believed in hell."

"I'm sure it was a figure of speech." I was suddenly very tired. "Get up, Anemone. Your liege is gone, and we've waited long enough for what we came for."

The sprite began wailing again. "COME BACK, MY QUEEN! COME BACK! YOU FORGOT ME!"

Gail rolled her eyes. "Oh, for God's sake. Get lost." She released her hold and the thing fell a couple of feet, frantically flapping her wings, before getting enough air under them to fly. She blew a tiny raspberry in Gail's face before winking out in a much smaller spray of glitter than Titania's.

"And don't bother us again," Gail called belatedly. Then she turned to Anemone, who was rising gracefully from the dirt. "Now. About the Air Key."

"It's not here," Anemone said promptly.

"You said it was," Gail said. "Where is it?"

"You can't reach it," the sylph said, pleased with herself. "I put it where you'll never be able to find it."

Collum, Rufus, and I exchanged a look. "The Otherworld," we said in unison.

"But *where* in the Otherworld?" Anemone said. Her tone was confident, but her eyes betrayed a bit of panic. Obviously we weren't supposed to guess her hidey-hole that fast. "It's a big place. Nobody knows everything about it."

16

"I bet we could get to it from here," Rufus said.

Collum nodded. "She didn't have enough time to be creative."

While the guys talked and Anemone looked increasingly alarmed, I glanced around for the cat. There she was, about ten feet away, standing on her hind legs and batting at something in the air. I walked toward her. "Did you find a bug? Or…" The closer I got, the more it was obvious what had caught her attention.

Collum told me once that he could find a gate he'd cut and sealed before just by looking for it. The fabric of reality looked slightly different there – you could see the seam. At the time, I'd had zero experience with Otherworld gates – fresh-cut or properly installed – and I couldn't see any of them. But we'd been traveling by gates fairly often over the past few weeks, and I guess my senses had become attuned or something. In any case, I realized what Tiger was batting at was a seam in the fabric of reality – hurriedly cut and even more hurriedly closed. It was short – maybe a foot long – and the edges didn't quite meet properly. In fact, they were kind of puckered.

"Go for it," I said quietly, when I got close enough.

"Hey!" Anemone yelled. "Get that cat away from there!"

Tiger extended a razor-sharp claw and neatly slit the seam.

"Nooooooooo!" Anemone wailed.

I reached through the gap and retrieved a bundle of windblown cloth.

Gail zipped up to me. "I'll take that," she said, and relieved me of the bundle. "Meet you at the car." I nodded decisively and she blew away.

Anemone screamed and stamped her foot. Then she flew off under her own wing power.

I picked up Tiger and rejoined the guys. "And they say *undines* are emotional. Wow."

"Must be the fae in her," Rufus said, deadpan.

"So now what?" asked Collum.

Now we thank the cat.

"Of course!" I said, nuzzling her neck. "Good Tiger! Good girl!"

She put her paws against my collarbone and pushed away. *Not like that. Stop it. Ugh!*

"Oh, shut up. You love it."

Rufus skritched her under the chin. "You were awesome. I mean it."

She began to purr.

Collum reached out and patted the top of her head. "Thanks, Tiger," he said. "Conor would be proud of you."

She opened her eyes wide and stared at him for a moment. Then she said, *I guess maybe you're okay.*

He and I shared a pleased grin. "Scratch her behind the ears," I said. "Yeah, like that. She loves it."

Traitor, Tiger said, but her purr got louder. *Now put me down.*

I let her jump down. "So how do we get back? Hiking down is easier than coming up, but…" I cast a meaningful look at the sky, where the sun was already heading toward the horizon. How much time had passed since we'd begun our trek up the mountain? I had no idea. And sunset would come sooner in the valleys below.

Collum was already bending to the task. "Who wants to go first?" he asked, indicating his newly-cut gate.

Tail up, Tiger waddled toward the gate. Just before she stepped through, she glanced back at me with eyes big and bright. *Don't forget – I get shrimp!*

CHAPTER 3 – TUESDAY IN THE SKY

We stepped out of the gate in the upper parking lot, next to the rental car. Not many cars had been parked there when we arrived, and now only two remained: ours and a beat-up pickup, its engine running. An elderly man in a flannel jacket sat inside. When he saw us, he opened the door and got out. That's when I realized he was Native American – his long gray braid swung around when he turned to shut the door.

"Hello," he called. "I heard there might be some trouble over here."

"Trouble? No, not at all," Collum said. "Where did you hear that?"

He gave us an inscrutable look. "Here and there."

Rufus raised an eyebrow. "Are you a cop or something?"

"Or something," the old man said with an odd smile. "My people have an ancient claim to this land. These mountains were our home once."

"Do you remember glaciers, too?" I blurted.

He turned a gimlet eye on me. "I am not quite that old." He paused, taking my measure. "You are the one who talked to the lake spirits." It wasn't a question.

Something about his manner made me trust him. "I am."

He nodded. "They spoke well of you." He kept nodding as he looked over the guys. "Of all of you." Then he pointed his chin toward the trailhead. "Did you see her up on the mountain?"

"Which one?" Collum said with a snort. "The sylph or the fairy queen?"

His mood darkened. "That one needs to go. This is not her land."

"Agreed," said Collum. "We sent her packing. Although I suspect we haven't seen the last of her."

"I think she's more interested in us than in this land," Rufus added.

The old man grunted in assent.

Rufus continued, "I think, once our business here is done, you will have seen the last of her."

"Sir," I broke in, "we're supposed to be meeting a friend here. She has gray hair and she's probably carrying a bundle of cloth. Have you seen her?"

He shook his head. "No. But I know where you can find her." He nodded toward the boulder road. "If you drive down to the campground, you will have an excellent view of the lakes. You will find her there."

"Thanks," said Collum. "We'll do that." He paused. "Uh, will you be okay here? It's going to be dark soon."

"I am waiting for my grandson. Do not worry. We have traveled this road many times together in the dark." An owl hooted nearby, and the old man nodded. "You should go now. Your friend may need your help."

We exchanged glances of alarm. "Thanks," Rufus said to the Native man. To us, he said, "Come on. Let's help Gail out of whatever jam she's in." We got in the SUV and Rufus fired it up. As he pulled out of the parking lot, we got an excellent view of the area where the old man's truck had been parked just a minute or two before. It was gone.

Collum frowned. "Did you see him leave?"

"Nope," Rufus said.

"People come and go so quickly here," I muttered. Then I braced myself for the bumpy trek down.

The campground, too, was deserted. We drove as far south as we could. The old man had been right – the vantage point gave us an awesome view of the Twin Lakes, the forebay behind us, and the mountains towering over us to the west.

Rufus pointed out over the lakes. "Is that...?"

It was. Gail and Anemone were whizzing and darting around one another, and it didn't look like they were playing around.

Sylphs, as a general rule, have wings. I've mentioned Anemone's large, lacy ones already. I'd never seen Gail's, as she always turned herself invisible before she buzzed off. In fact, until now I would have sworn she didn't have any.

Yeah, no, she did. They weren't anywhere near as pretty as Anemone's, but they were awesome in their own right, with what looked like some kind of shiny, flexible metal in place of the lace. They appeared sharper, more dangerous. More like military-grade weaponry.

In fact, Anemone appeared to be bleeding.

"What are they fighting over? I asked.

"Where's the Key?" Collum asked at the same time. And honestly, his question was more pertinent.

"She doesn't appear to be carrying it," Rufus said. "She must have stashed it somewhere."

We exchanged a quick glance. Now where would Gail have stashed that bundle?

"Tiger!" I called to the cat, who had sauntered out from under the nearest dumpster. "Did you happen to see… What have you got in your mouth?"

Dinner. She dropped the limp, furry thing to the ground and began batting at it to get it to move again.

"Is that a *rat?*" I said. "Eww! How could you?"

Somebody's gonna have to rustle up dinner, and you people are pathetic at hunting.

"Honestly," I said, and then stopped. It was pointless. Tiger was a cat. She was going to do cat things. In fact, I was kind of proud of her for catching anything, as portly as she was. So I changed tack. "Did you happen to see what Gail did with the thing we retrieved from the Otherworld?"

Mmm. Yeah. She batted at the formerly alive thing several times, sitting on her haunches as if ready to run should it move.

"Where did she put it?"

Under the car.

I cast her a dubious look, then got down on all fours to inspect the undercarriage.

Not under *under. Inside under.* She sighed a kitty sigh and left her prey to join me at the car.

"What do you mean, inside under?"

Under the thing in the back of the car. Here, open that door.

"You mean the hatch?"

Whatever. Just get on with it, sister. My meal isn't getting any fresher.

I popped open the hatch and peered inside. Nothing here but the tents and ground cloths, my ginormous pack, the bag with the freeze-dried food in it, and...

I thought hard. Under something, but inside.

I pushed some of our stuff around and noticed a tattered corner of cloth sticking out of a crack in the flooring. I pulled at the edge of flooring and it came up just enough for me to see what was beneath it: the teeny-tiny spare tire, the standard-issue useless jack, and a lump of rotted cloth.

"Guys?" I said. "It's here. It's in with the spare."

"How?" Rufus asked, coming over to look. "I had the key fob."

"Magic!" Collum said, fluttering his fingers as if casting a spell. "Get in. Let's get down there and give her a lift." He pulled open the driver's side door as he spoke.

Rufus tossed him the fob and got in the passenger's seat. I climbed in back. "Come on, Tiger!" I yelled. "Leave that nasty thing right there!"

It's gone. Must have been playing possum. Stupid humans distracted me. She groused all the way to the SUV. Then she sat, looking up at the seat as if calculating the coefficient of something-or-other.

"Oh, for God's sake," I said. I got out, picked her up, and practically threw her inside. "We need to *go.*"

I was going, she said in a wounded tone, and commenced licking her fur furiously.

Collum shook his head and we lurched forward.

In a few minutes we were back on flatland and cruising past the lakes. Rufus rolled down his window, stuck most of the upper half of his body out, and whistled. "Retreat!" he yelled. "Retreat!"

Gail got the message. With a final swoop, the edge of her right wing sliced through the bottom left lobe of Anemone's. The sylph cried out in pain, then spun earthward, her tattered wing flapping uselessly in the breeze.

Gail stayed aloft long enough to make sure her opponent was down for the count. Then she disapparated and materialized inside the car next to me. "Go! Go! Go!" she yelled. Collum obliged.

At the T-intersection with U.S. 24, he turned left. "We're going to Leadville?" Rufus asked.

"Through it. And all the way to I-70," said Collum. "This is the way we would have come in, if that snip of a... Good Neighbor... hadn't scared us with that bogus avalanche danger sign and made us go out of our way."

Mentally, I applauded his caution. The last thing we needed was to invite that sprite to come after us again.

"Is the Key still where I put it?" Gail asked.

Rufus turned all the way around in his seat to look at her. "Yeah, and how did you get it into the car when I had the car key?"

She smiled mysteriously but said nothing. He stared at her, incredulous, for at least a minute, but her smile only widened. Finally, he threw up his hands and faced forward again.

"Did you see the old guy at the parking lot?" I asked her.

"What old guy?"

"That nice old Native American guy in the pickup truck."

She eyed me. "There wasn't anybody in the lot when I got back. Are you saying someone was watching me?"

I heard suspicion in her tone and tried to calm her down. "Hey. I don't think he was dangerous. He did tell us where to find you, though, so I thought maybe you'd... No, huh?"

"No." She scanned the road behind us.

"Gail," Collum said. "Look at me." When she had made eye contact with him in the rear-view mirror, he said, "There was nothing nefarious about him. He talked a lot about how his people had the original claim to the land. I think he's a guardian, kind of, of his tribe's sacred places."

"He told you that," she said.

"Not in so many words, but that was the impression I got. And don't forget," he said, "I have an affinity for the Earth myself. I'd know if he was lying about it."

She considered his words. "Okay," she said at last, and we all relaxed.

Until we got to Leadville, when everybody's cellphones went off at once.

Collum found a parking space on the main drag near the Tabor Opera House. "I guess we're back in civilization," he said, fishing his phone out of his pocket.

"That's odd," Gail said. "I got a text from Ben Gelber." She looked up. "You remember him, right? We Skyped with him at Collum's parents' house."

I did remember him. He was a rabbi and an expert on folklore and mythology. Gail had met him through work at the spy agency she couldn't tell us about.

"Does he have more information about the Keys?" Collum asked. "Or the Tool?"

"He must," she said. "He wants me to meet him in L.A. as soon as possible."

"Well, that's convenient," said Rufus. "Annie emailed me. She and Auntie Helen are coming to the mainland to visit relatives. They're supposed to arrive at LAX tomorrow."

Collum looked up at him, a curious expression on his face. "Really? Because my parents are also on their way to L.A."

"That's great!" I said. "I can put everybody up at the beach house. I have tons of room, and I'd love for you guys to see it."

"Don't you think it's weird, though?" Rufus asked me. "That everybody's showing up at once?"

I shrugged. "Coincidences happen, you know?"

24

"What's your message, Raney?" Collum asked.

"Oh! Right. I forgot." I fiddled with my phone. "I have two voicemails from Mam. No, three. All within the last couple of days." I laughed shortly. "Talk about odd. She *never* calls me."

"Put the messages on speaker," Gail urged.

"Sure. Here's the first one." I hit play.

"Raney? It's your mother. Just letting you know that I'm locking up Conor's house and leaving the key in the shed next to the… you know." I did know. There was a permanent gate into the Otherworld in that shed. "Tiger's gone off I don't know where, but I'm not worried. I have a feeling she can take care of herself."

I hit pause and toed the cat with my shoe. She looked up at me sleepily. *She's nice. I like her.*

"Right. You like her so much that you left without a word."

I knew she'd figure it out. Tiger closed her eyes and drifted off again.

I shook my head and hit play again. "I'm going to head out to your place. I've been seeing some scary things on the news about wildfires in California and I think someone ought to be there to keep an eye on the house."

"Wildfires?" I said, sitting up straighter.

"That does sound scary," Collum said.

"Yeah," I said, panic closing in. "That's the first one. Here's the second." I opened that one and hit play.

"Raney, it's your mother. I'm here and the house is fine. I'm going to stay, though, until the danger is past. Call me back, would you?"

"That's reassuring," said Rufus.

"Yeah, not really," I said, frowning. "She never asks me to call her. It almost sounds like it's in code – like things really aren't okay but she doesn't want to put it in a voicemail."

"There's one more, right?" said Collum.

"Yeah," I said with a nervous laugh. Mam's messages were doing a good job of scaring me.

"Raney, where are you? The fires are getting closer. Something's not right about this. Please come home as soon as you can."

I stared at the phone. "She sounds scared. Mam's never scared." I looked up wildly. "I've got to get home."

"Call her back," Gail said.

"Oh, right." I dialed her cell phone number. It rang and rang. At last it went to voicemail. "Hi, Mam. It's Raney. We're in Colorado. I just now got all of your messages. I'll be home very soon." I swallowed. "Please call me back, okay?" I ended the call and looked at my teammates – no, my friends. "I've got to get home right now."

"But we need to take the rental car back," Collum said.

"And return a bunch of this gear we didn't use," said Gail. I remembered it had gone on her credit card. I didn't want her to lose all that money, but panic was setting in.

"I can go alone," I said. "You guys take all the stuff back and meet me as soon as you can."

Nothing doing, sister, Tiger said. She jumped up into my lap.

Gail said, "Remember when you asked Collum's father where the Door was? Remember what he said?"

You bet I remembered. He'd given me the strangest look and said, *You of all people should know the answer to that.* "But I didn't know what he meant," I said. "I still don't know."

"Raney," Collum said gently. "Think, sweetheart. Your father has three of the Keys."

"*Surgat* has them," I corrected.

"Sure, okay, Surgat. Or whoever he answers to. But we have the fourth one. And they're not going to give up until they get it from us."

"But Damien's trapped in a volcanic rift," I said.

"Not forever," said Rufus. "And Surgat had a powerful motivation to find his way out."

"Okay, but if they've escaped, why aren't they here, chasing us?" I argued.

26

"Why chase your prey when you can lure them right to you?" Gail said.

That's a pretty smart strategy, Tiger said. *Humans may get the hang of hunting yet.*

I hardly heard the cat's thought-talk. I'd gone cold all over. "So my mother is at my house, and Damien is there, too?" I unbuckled my seat belt. "He'll catch her again, and it will be all my fault! Let me out!" In a single, fluid movement, I threw open the door and slid out. "I've got to go home!"

In less than a moment, Collum was beside me. "Not alone," he said. "Not without us."

"But..."

"I *can't* let you go alone! He wants *you,* too!"

The anguish in his voice got through to me. My rock-solid gnome was *emoting.* I threw my arms around his neck and held on.

"It's a trap, Raney," I heard Rufus say. "Your mother is the bait."

"They're baiting all of us," Gail said. "Collum's parents, Annie and Auntie Helen, Ben..." Her voice caught. She cleared her throat and went on, "Everybody's converging on L.A."

"On Malibu. Where the Door is," I said bitterly into Collum's collar. Rationally, it was the only thing that made sense, but my emotions had yet to catch up. I straightened and faced them all. "How could it be, though? I should have known, or felt it, or something!"

"We're going to find out," Gail said. "Come on. The sooner we get back to Denver, the sooner we end this."

CHAPTER 4 – TUESDAY IN A FOG

I doubt you'll be surprised to hear that we got back to Denver a lot quicker than it had taken us to get to Twin Lakes. Traffic was light and the weather was beautiful. I might even have enjoyed the mountain scenery if I hadn't been so queasy about getting back home *now now NOW*.

I'd been away for too long. I was never going to stay away for so long again. Well, maybe to go on location for a film or something, but that was *it*.

I hoped Mam was okay. I hoped Damien hadn't found her. I hoped he was still trapped in that volcanic maze Collum had created. Maybe most of all, I hoped my beach house – my forever home – was still standing.

I felt a little guilty when I realized that I cared more about my house than about my mother. But I knew Mam could take care of herself – I mean, she'd been taking care of the two of us for as long as I could remember. She had brains and cunning, and resources of her own. If worse came to worst, she could jump straight off my pool deck into the Pacific and swim away. She'd find her undine family eventually, and she could stay with them until Damien died of old age. There was nothing keeping *him* alive past a normal span of mortal years. Hosting a demon wasn't enough to make one magical.

No, if things got too hot for Mam, she could save herself.

But she wouldn't. Because of me.

I didn't have an undine family to take me in. We'd always lived apart from her people. Mam's rationale, I thought, was the less they knew of my existence, the safer I'd be. I mean, I was just guessing – maybe she had a different reason. Maybe Damien hadn't been blowing smoke when he said Mam's family wouldn't take her back. Group dynamics are just as complicated among Elementals are they are among humans, Collum's dysfunctional family being Exhibit A.

Why had Damien told me all that stuff about his parents, anyway? I'd never given a thought to my father's side of the family, but now I was curious about them. None of the bios of my father that I'd found online had ever mentioned his childhood, past a recitation of his parents' names and where they'd lived. He must have engineered that. So why bother telling me that my DNA was more tainted than I knew? *Lester and Sharyn Jones,* he'd said. *A mother who couldn't love anybody and a father whom I could never please. Be glad you never met them.*

As high-society as they'd been, the local newspapers must have published their obituaries. I was tempted to pull out my phone and google them, just to see whether everyone thought they were as horrid as Damien portrayed them, but the cellphone signal wasn't fabulous in the mountains and the search would probably be more frustrating than just sitting here and stewing.

"How close are we?" I asked. I'd been so lost in my own thoughts that I hadn't followed any of the chit-chat in the car, and I'd barely noticed when we stopped at a rest area to switch drivers. Now Rufus was at the wheel and Collum was next to me in back.

"She speaks!" Rufus cried.

Collum grinned and took my hand. "You've been so quiet that we wondered if you'd gone catatonic."

"Just thinking," I said. "Chewing things over." *Trying to keep my mind off what's happening in Malibu.*

"Speaking of chewing, is anybody hungry?" Rufus said.

I was promised shrimp, Tiger said from her spot on the floor at my feet.

"You don't count," Collum told her. "You're always hungry."

Hmpf. Tiger lashed her tail, whacking my ankles.

"Hey now," I said, making a weak attempt at a grin. "If you're mad at him, don't hit *me.*"

"I could use something to drink," Gail said. "Raney?"

I swallowed a sigh. "How close are we?"

"About twenty minutes out."

"I can wait."

"I knew she'd say that," Rufus groused. "You had to ask her, didn't you, Gail?"

"You can live off the fat of the land for twenty more minutes," she said with a smile.

"Are you calling me fat?" he said in mock anger.

I was glad we were all getting along, but really, I just wanted to be out of the car, shed of the car and the extra gear, and heading through one of Collum's gates.

It was dark by the time we got downtown. The outfitter's place was still open and was happy to buy back our unused gear. While Gail attended to that, Collum and I returned the car.

Of course, the place was closed. Tears of frustration leaked from my eyes. "We're going to have to stay another day, aren't we?"

"Of course not. They have a key drop next to the door – see?" He pointed to the slot in the wall. "Let's get this beast unloaded."

The slight physical activity helped calm me down. By the time we had everything on the curb and the key in the slot, Gail and Rufus had joined us.

"Okay, food," Rufus said.

Collum pulled out his phone. "What's your pleasure? Sushi, Mexican, burgers…?"

"Diner?" Rufus asked hopefully.

Collum consulted the list. "Sam's Number Three," he said. "This way."

We had walked about half a block, laden with our baggage, when Collum stopped. "It's several more blocks," he said. "Or we could take a shortcut."

"Shortcut," the rest of us chorused. And so it was that we made the trek from Union Station to the diner in record time.

As chatty as everyone had been in the car, now that we were in a place where we could relax a little, we seemed to have run out of conversation. I mean, maybe the others were going inside themselves, reaching for their last reserves of strength before we met our greatest challenge or whatever. Me? I was exhausted. Just in the last twenty-four hours, we'd survived an epic drive, fought off a crazed sylph, climbed a fourteener (well, most of it), gotten the best of the queen of the Fair Folk, and dealt with an annoying fairy twice. And Gail had done aerial combat with that same crazed sylph. I could barely remember lunch, let alone breakfast. Wading in the South Platte River seemed like a lifetime ago.

But for once, we'd gotten what we came for. "Hey, guys," I said. "We got the Air Key."

Tired smiles all around.

"You know," Rufus said, "it's hard to believe we've been through so much in so short a time."

"It hasn't even been six weeks," said Gail. She was right.

"I think I'd like to come back to Colorado," I said. "But I'd like to stay longer next time."

That got a chuckle from everyone. We hadn't even been here a full day.

At about that point, the food showed up. As soon as I smelled it, I realized I was famished. I ended up cleaning my plate. So did Collum and Gail. Rufus had to place a second order – there wasn't anything left to filch from us.

"Hey," Collum said as we were finishing up, "you know what we haven't seen here in Colorado?"

"Nope." That was Rufus.

"Any of Surgat's clay buddies."

"That's right," said Gail. "Maybe he didn't have enough time to make more, after the aumakua destroyed so many at Loihi."

"I'm not saying I'm sorry about it, to be clear," Collum said.

"I'm not, either," I said, shuddering. "I was the one submerged in an Irish bog, trying to fend off two of them alone. Thank goodness that fellow from the Tuatha showed up to help."

"Don't give him so much credit," Collum said. "You outdid yourself." He looked around the table. "We've all outdone ourselves. Every one of us has done heroic things. Don't forget that."

That sounded like a cue, so I slid out of the booth. "Time to get moving again," I said. "I think I might have another heroic deed or two in me."

"Heroes," Gail said with a wondrous smile.

Rufus slapped the table. "You bet we are."

As we gathered by the door to leave the restaurant, Collum said, "So what do you think the chances are that we'll get any sleep tonight?"

I thought of what we were about to walk into: friends and family members, each with their own claims on us; the Door and the unknown evil behind it; my father and his demon, and probably whoever was behind the demon; and a fire, or something worse, threatening the home I loved.

Plus we'd lose an hour going west. It might still be light there. We might be in time to catch the sun's final glimmerings on the waves before it sank beneath the sea.

"Zero," I said. "Zero chances that we'll be getting any sleep any time soon."

"That's what I thought," he said. He made his way over to cashier. "Hey, do you guys carry energy drinks? You know, those little five-hour bottles? Sweet. We'll take a case."

CHAPTER 5 – TUESDAY EVENING, HERE AND THERE AND ALSO KIND OF THERE

My mother used to sing me a song about how it never rained in southern California. It was an enchanting idea at the time, but I can tell you now that it's not true. It doesn't rain often, but it does sometimes.

Still, the thought of sunshine and surf was super-attractive to me when I was growing up. It's part of why I settled there. Okay, the film industry is there, too, but that just made it seem all the more perfect.

It was warm and sunny when I saw my house in Malibu for the first time. And since then, I've seen my neighborhood in a lot of different moods: bright sunshine, chilly fog, and yes, sometimes clouds and rain. But I'd never seen it the way I did when we arrived that night.

We missed the sunset by about twenty minutes, but I'm not sure we would have been able to see much anyway. Ominous clouds filled the sky, from just above our heads to the horizon. Thunder crackled now and then, and the surf crashed continuously against the rocks.

My pool deck is a perfect vantage point for watching the sunset. The sea and sky seem to catch fire as the sun heads to bed. But on this night, the only fire we could see was an unnatural one burning in the hills to the northwest. It seemed to march toward us as we stood there agape, defying the turbulent wind blowing hard off the ocean.

"How is that possible?" Gail murmured. "The wind is from the west. The fire shouldn't be coming this way at all."

"I bet we'll find the answer when we find the demon," Collum said.

"Sooner than that," Rufus said. "Look." He pointed to the nearest hillcrest, where a giant man-shaped creature lumbered, step after mechanical step. Fire bloomed in its wake.

A hysterical giggle escaped me. "So that's where the golems got to," I said. Then I cleared my throat, got a grip, and turned toward the ocean again. "My place is down there." I started walking home and the rest of the team followed me.

We didn't get far. "Halt!" a voice boomed from the darkness. "L.A. County sheriff! This is a restricted area!"

"Oh, sorry, deputy," I said, turning up the wattage on my smile. "I'm Raney Meadows. I live on Broad Beach Road." I took off my ginormous backpack and began fishing around in a side pocket for my driver's license.

"That's okay," he said. "I don't need to see your ID, Ms. Meadows – I recognize you. But I can't let you through the security cordon. There's a mandatory evacuation order in place. It's not safe in this area right now."

"Evacuation?" I said faintly. "But my mother's staying at my house. She's been housesitting while I've been away – on location – for the past several weeks." I was ad libbing as fast as I could. "She called me just a little while ago, but she didn't say anything about evacuating. Can't I just go down there and check on her? And make sure my house is still standing?"

"I wish I could let you, but I have my orders. You understand."

"Sure, of course," I said, hoping I sounded dazed with shock. "But how do I find my mother? Do you know where she is?"

"No, ma'am, I don't, and no one out here on the perimeter would know, either. We kind of have our hands full with this fire."

"Of course," I said again.

"The Red Cross has a shelter set up at Malibu High School. You might try looking for her there."

"Okay. I mean, I will. Thanks."

He saluted as I walked away, the others trailing after me into the dark.

"Wonderful," Gail said, her mouth twisted in frustration. "Now what do we do?"

In answer, Collum cut a gate. Then he waved me toward it. "Take us home, Raney."

I smiled gratefully and stepped through. Then I stopped.

This wasn't the instantaneous kind of gate – instead it was a doorway into that parallel world that's just a click or two off from ours. In this world, Malibu was quieter, wilder, and much less populated. The hills weren't aflame and the sky was clear, blue deepening to black as the first stars became visible above us. The air smelled like the sea. I could hear gentle waves lapping at the cliffs.

"It's so beautiful. And the stars are the same," I marveled.

"More or less," Collum said. "There are some differences, but you'd need a telescope to see them." He motioned toward the beach. "Is that your place?"

"Oh," I breathed. It sure looked like my house, but what was it doing here? I took a few steps toward it, then broke into a run.

The gate was the same, the walkway was the same, even the front door was the same – right down to the dolphin-shaped door knocker. The security keypad was missing – I guess that technology didn't work here – but the doorknob had a lock and I had the key. I fitted it in and turned, and the door swung open.

"Hello?" someone called from inside.

"Mam!" I dropped my stuff just inside the door and ran to my mother's arms. "Oh, thank God you're all right. Your messages scared me – and then that sheriff's deputy told me I couldn't go home…" I let go and burst into tears. It had been a ridiculously long day, jam-packed with enough crazy happenings to last an average week, and I was running on very little sleep. In that kind of situation, blubbering is what I do best.

Mam patted me on the back and let me cry it out. When I'd wound down to snuffling, she said over my shoulder, "Hello, Collum. Nice to see you again."

I sprang away from her. "Sorry. I should introduce you to my friends. This is Gail Oleander, our sylph. Gail, this is my mother."

Gail stepped forward and offered her hand. "It's a pleasure to meet you," she said.

Mam smiled and shook.

"And come to think of it, you've met Rufus already."

"Yes, I have. Nice to see you."

Rufus smiled and nodded. "Uh, ma'am? What should we call you? 'Ms. Raney's mother' doesn't exactly roll off the tongue."

Mam laughed. "You may call me Ondine. Would you like anything to eat or drink? I know Rufus's answer already…" We shared a laugh at his expense. But I mean, Mam wasn't wrong. "But what about the rest of you?" She led the way to my kitchen and flipped on the light.

I was startled. "How… Where's the electricity coming from?"

"I wondered the same thing," she said. "The house must still be connected to our world somehow."

"I've heard of that happening," Collum said, helping himself to a glass and some ice.

"Oh, yeah – make yourselves at home, guys," I said. "Wow. I'm a lousy hostess today."

"You've been through a lot," said Gail, taking a seat at the breakfast bar. "We all have."

"Water, Gail?" asked Collum.

She waved him off. "I'm good for now, thanks."

Rufus, of course, was rummaging through the fridge.

I turned back to my mother. "But what's my house doing *here*?"

She sat on another stool at the bar. "That's a good question. When I arrived, of course, it was in our world, or I wouldn't have been able to find it. Then the weather began to deteriorate. The wind came up out of nowhere. And then those horrible clay men showed up and started patrolling the streets. Last night, the fires started." She shivered. "I was so frightened I could hardly sleep."

"I thought you might…" I hooked a thumb over my shoulder and mimed a dive off the side of a pool – or in this case, over a cliff.

She nodded. "The thought occurred to me. But I finally nodded off, and when I woke up, the ocean was calm and everything seemed to be back to normal. It wasn't until I looked out the kitchen window that I realized the house had moved during the night."

"To protect itself," said Collum. "I've heard of that, too."

"Your cabin in Harpers Ferry," I said. "Can it do that?"

"Among other things." I was tempted to ask him for specifics, but he kept talking. "Typically, it's not the house that's enchanted, but the earth it's built on."

Gail sat forward, her chin propped on her hand. "I've never heard of this before. What triggers it?"

"Usually, extreme danger."

"Well, our current situation qualifies," I said with a sigh. I glanced at the pile of food on Rufus's plate. "Seriously, dude? We ate less than two hours ago."

For once, he looked embarrassed. "I'll put some of it back."

"No, it's fine. It's just... Leave something for breakfast, okay? I have no idea where the nearest grocery store is."

"We can get to one," Collum said, "but we'll have to dodge the sheriff's blockade. Here, let me have some of that." He nabbed some crackers and cheese from Rufus's plate.

"So we can move pretty freely between this world and our own? Huh. Yeah, I guess we can, considering that's how your cabin is set up. Right?"

Collum's mouth was full, so he could only nod. He swallowed and said, "My only question is whether any of the house is still showing in our world – and if it is, how much."

"You think we're straddling realities?" said Rufus. "Interesting."

"It stands to reason," Collum said. "We're still getting power."

"What about the fire, then?" I said, fear creeping up my backbone. "Could it reach us here?"

Collum shook his head. "I wish I knew. Da would know, but... Oh." He pulled out his handy-dandy pocket computer, stared at it for a moment, and made a face.

"No signal?" said Rufus.

"Nope." Collum put his phone back in his pants pocket. "And we have folks coming to meet us. We're going to have to go back to our world to get them – there's no way to get anyone a message from here."

Gail tapped her chin with a forefinger. "Your father can cut gates, too, right?"

"Right."

"Okay. I have an idea." She leaned her forearms on the breakfast bar. "How about the three of us go back to our world and send messages to everyone? Tell them all to meet here. No, wait. They'll have to meet somewhere outside the security cordon."

"There's a Pavilions grocery store," I said, and gave her the address. "Then what?"

"They send us a signal when everyone has arrived, and we go out to meet them and bring them here."

"How can they get a signal to us?" said Rufus.

Collum said, "Da can get to the house and cut the power. We'll have to leave a lamp on so we know when the power's off. Raney, where's the breaker box?"

"The what?" I said.

He stared at me. "You don't know where your breaker box is?"

I shot him an incredulous look. "Of course not. If something breaks, I have people to call."

While Collum kept staring, Rufus said, "We can find it. Where's your HVAC system?"

"My what?"

He tried again. "What about your water heater?"

"Oh. That's an on-demand thing. I paid big bucks for it, too." I grinned.

"Okay, but where is it?"

I squinted and looked at the ceiling. I honestly didn't know where any of this stuff was. I had a maintenance guy on speed dial and a pool cleaner who came once a week.

38

"Let's start looking," Collum said. Rufus nodded and pulled open the doors to the cabinet under the sink.

I'll do it. Tiger appeared in the kitchen window as if she'd been sitting there all along.

We all turned to her. "You'll do what?" Rufus said.

I'll go get the troops and bring them here.

I looked at her dubiously. "You think you can find the Pavilions?"

She turned her unblinking stare on me. *Do they sell tuna there? Then I can find it.*

"That makes a certain amount of sense," Rufus said. He shut the cabinet doors. "Okay, then, we need to go back for a few minutes to send our messages."

"We should limit our exposure there," Gail said. "Let's write the messages here, before we make the transition."

"Good idea," said Collum, pulling out his phone again. He paused and looked at me. "But while we're there, let's make time to see how much of the house is visible. And where the fire is."

"Sounds like a plan," said Gail, and went to get her tablet from her luggage.

I walked over to Collum and hugged him. "Thank you."

He kissed my forehead, then my lips. "I know you're worried. If it were my place in danger, I'd be going nuts."

I kissed him back, then set him free. "So, uh, while you guys are back in the real world, sending your messages, I guess I'll make up the guest rooms." I gave them a half-hearted smile. "If you bring me back good news, we might get some sleep tonight, after all."

CHAPTER 6 – WHAT TIME IS IT, ANYWAY?

One thing about doing housework – it frees up your mind to think. Although sometimes thinking turns into overthinking, and that's maybe worse than not thinking at all.

Maybe that's why Buddhist monks are always talking about clearing your mind and staying in the present moment. Focusing on the now doesn't leave room for overthinking.

Anyway, I was trying to focus on the now while making up all the guest beds. There's a system to it: pull off the bedspread, get the linens from the closet, put on the sheets, stuff the pillowcases with pillows, put on a fresh bedspread, leave extra blankets and pillows where they'll be handy, leave a chocolate on the pillow, move to the next room. My beach house had six bedrooms, plus the living room sofa in a pinch, and we were going to be pretty well pinched. Mam had already staked out the room she always used when visiting me. I figured Collum would be with me in the master suite, his parents would have a room together, Annie and her mother could have the room with two twin beds, and Gail and Rufus would each have their own rooms. That left Ben Gelber the sofa. But I had a feeling things would sort themselves out: if Annie stayed with Rufus, and if my mother and Annie's mother bunked together, then Gelber could have a room, too.

I mean, I wasn't going to make the suggestion. I figured it would happen on its own. And either way, everybody would have a place to sleep.

But just to be safe, I suggested to Mam that she make up the other twin bed in her room. She didn't ask why. Maybe she'd been doing some overthinking of her own.

Anyway, once that was settled, there was nothing left to do but menial work. And think. Or overthink.

The golems were here – well, here in our world – so that meant Surgat and my father had found their way out of Collum's volcanic maze. But it must have kept them busy long enough that there was no point for them to head back to Twin Lakes. Or maybe they had, and discovered they'd missed us.

But that made no sense in terms of timing. Damien would have had to get back to Denver to return that big, black SUV and whoever was driving it. Then he would have had to catch a flight to LAX, and get from there to Malibu, and have enough time for Surgat to whip up some golems to start the fires.

Which had started before we got here. And Mam already knew something was up by the time she left her second message.

No, once Surgat unlocked Collum's device, he and Damien must have hightailed it here.

Which meant they must have figured out how to travel by gate.

Although Surgat probably already knew how. After all, he'd been leaving Damien temporarily to hand over each Key to his master. Maybe he simply hadn't known how to transport a non-magical human. Or he'd known how but hadn't bothered. Or his master hadn't wanted him to.

Regardless, if Surgat and Damien had made it to Malibu via the Otherworld – and that was the only thing that made sense, given the timing – then it meant they might be able to find my house.

That sent a cold chill up my back. I'd thought we were safe here, at least for tonight, and maybe longer. Maybe until the fire in our world literally cut the cord that was keeping the house tied there.

But if Surgat could navigate to this world... or if there were a way to follow the electrical connection here...

I was able to finish making all the beds, even though my hands were shaking.

Then I tried to stuff down my fear by checking all of the guest bathrooms, wiping down all the counters and making sure each one had soap and toiletries and fresh towels.

I also cleaned all the toilets and swept the floors.

I was about to break out the vacuum cleaner when I heard a babble of voices in the living room. I rushed out to greet the team and realized the guests had arrived, too – or most of them, anyway. Niall and Kate Barth were chatting with Collum, Annie and Rufus looked like they'd glued themselves to one another, and Mam and Auntie Helen were already in an animated conversation. Tiger was curled up on the sofa with her eyes half-closed.

Gail stood apart, arms crossed.

"Hi, everyone, and welcome," I said. "Glad it all worked out."

"Sorry it took so long," Collum said, giving me a hug. "When we found out everyone's planes had already landed, we decided to wait for Tiger to fetch them. Hope we didn't worry you."

"Nope, not worried. Or anyway, not about that."

"Oh? What is it?"

"Well, it occurred to me that Surgat has probably figured out how to get Damien through the Otherworld. I mean, how else did they beat us here?"

"Okay."

"So that means Surgat can come here. *Here* here." I pointed at the floor for emphasis. "This specific universe where the house is hiding."

Niall smiled. "I'd be pleased to explain it all someday, Raney, but that's not something to be worried about."

"Yeah?" I said, pulling away from Collum. "Why not?"

"Because the land here is enchanted," he said. "It knew when to hide, and it also knew where to go. If this place becomes too dangerous, the land will move it again."

I crossed my arms. "Yeah? You're sure about that?" I looked from father to son.

"I'm dead certain," said Niall.

Collum shrugged. "It's how our cottage works. I assume it's the same here. And anyway, I believe Da."

"There you go, see?" said Niall with a self-satisfied smile.

I wasn't completely satisfied, but I was willing to let the matter drop for the moment. I turned to Gail. "So where's Mr. Gelber?"

"He's been delayed," she said acidly.

"Sounds like you don't believe him," Rufus said with a grin.

Gail dropped her arms to her sides and paced to the windows overlooking the pool. "This isn't the first time he's pulled this. There's always just one more question to look up, or one more detail to chase down. And then I'm left to do the hard work myself." She paced back. "I hate working with academics."

"Well, you won't be alone this time," I said.

She stopped cold and looked at me, surprised. Then her features softened. "That's right," she said. "Thanks, Raney."

"You're welcome. Now, I don't want to be a party pooper, but…" I stifled a yawn.

Mam realized where I was going and had a question of her own. "But how safe would we be, if we went to sleep? We're told the house is still connected to our world. What's the situation there?"

"How close is the fire?" I asked. "And how much of the house is visible?"

"We checked all that out while we were waiting," Rufus said. "The house looks like it's there, but it's warded. We all got the sense it would be a bad idea for us to get near it."

"Really? That's not how I left it." I turned to Mam. "Did you do that?"

It was me. Tiger cracked an eyelid. *Nobody else seemed to think of it, so I did it.*

"Now that you mention it," Rufus said with a crooked grin, "the wards did feel oddly catlike."

I remembered the last time I'd run into one of Tiger's wards. "You didn't put a bucket of water over the gate, did you?"

Very funny. She stretched and sighed, then curled up again. *It didn't work last time, so no.*

43

"Good. Thank you."

Don't mention it. In fact, all of you could shut up so I could sleep.

"We'll take that under advisement," Collum said cheerfully. "As for the fire, it's well away from your neighborhood, the wind has died down, and the golems seem to have disappeared for now. I think it will be okay for us to get some shuteye."

"We could set a watch, if you want," Rufus said. "I can take the first couple of hours."

"That's silly," I said. "Who can find us here?"

Someone knocked on the door.

Everyone froze except Gail. "Well, we know it's not Surgat," she said. "He'd bust right in."

"Maybe it's Mr. Gelber," I said, heading for the door. "I mean, who else could it be?"

The knock sounded again before I got to the door. "Coming," I called. Two steps more and I reached the peephole. I stood on tiptoe to look out, cursing myself anew for never having it moved lower on the door. Then I rocked back in shock.

Collum came up behind me. "Raney?"

Our visitor knocked a third time. "Fine, fine," I muttered. "How much weirder can it get?" I opened the door.

There on my threshold stood Allen Owings of the *Sentinel*, the newspaper in Harpers Ferry, West Virginia.

He looked as surprised as I felt. Then he cleared his throat. "Raney Meadows? I'm Allen Owings, of…"

"Yeah, I remember you. Hi, Allen."

"Oh. That's… That's great. Because I'd like to ask you some questions."

I sighed. "When have you not?" I said, gesturing toward the living room. "Come on in and join the party."

He got three or four feet in before he was stopped short by my favorite gnome. Collum had clearly been practicing his bad-guy stance; he assumed it now – shoulders squared, arms crossed – and said, "We have a few questions for you, too. For starters, how did you get here?"

I swung my arms underhand, palms up. "Let's all head for the living room, where we'll be more comfortable. Allen, you need anything to drink?"

"No thank you, I'm fine. Oh." He stopped again, surveying the roomful of people staring at him. "You really are having a party."

"We were just on our way to bed, actually," Rufus said. "Aren't you the newspaper reporter who published all those photos of us at Lost Falls?"

"And got Raney fired?" Collum said.

He looked so mortified that I almost forgave him. "I owe you an apology, Ms. Meadows. I never realized the impact my scoop would have on your career."

"Yeah, well, it would have been fine if you hadn't spread the photos all over social media," I said caustically. "Anyway, what are you doing here? Malibu isn't in the *Sentinel's* circulation area, is it?"

"I don't work for the *Sentinel* anymore," he said, puffing out his chest. "I'm working for the Associated Press now."

"Congratulations," I snarled. "Why are you here?"

My tone of voice put him off his stride. What did he expect me to do, thank him for everything he'd done for me? "Well, uh," he said as he recovered, "I'm covering the fires for the AP, and I got a tip that something unnatural was setting them."

"So you immediately thought of us," Gail said. "How touching."

"Not at first," he said. "But then I found out Ms. Meadows's house was here…"

"So you came over to say hi?" I said. "Or to blame us for the fires?"

He sat down in the closest chair. "Look, it's no secret that weird stuff seems to happen around you people. First there was the situation at Harpers Ferry…"

Rufus interrupted him. "How's my old pal Alex Drake doing, anyway?"

Allen blinked. "Okay, I guess. I heard he's donated his fortune to clean up the Chesapeake Bay." He didn't stay sidetracked for long, though. "Then I heard about something involving a processing plant in Ireland. It makes mulch or something."

"Peat," Niall corrected. "The plant processes peat. The Irish have used it to heat their homes for generations."

"Peat, right," Allen said. "And you are...?"

"Niall Barth, Collum's father. This is my wife Kate."

Allen got up and shook hands with them politely, then sat back down. "Anyway, I found out the four of you were there at the time..." He paused as he looked between Collum and his parents.

"We were visiting my parents," Collum offered. "To bring them my dead brother's things."

Allen gulped, but forged ahead. "And then I learned that you were in Hawaii a few days ago when a new volcano erupted out of the ocean..."

"We were on vacation," I said. "Rufus has family there."

"And here they are," he said. "Helen Yamamoto and her daughter Annie."

Allen got up again to shake hands. His theory was falling apart before his eyes, but he pressed on. "But then I learned about the fire here in Malibu, and Ms. Meadows's house being here..."

"You mentioned that already," I said. "And you forgot Colorado."

"Colorado?"

"Yeah. We were there yesterday." I sat across from him. "So you're thinking we're *responsible* for all of this? Alex Drake's transformation, and the industrial whatever-it-was in Ireland, and..." I laughed for effect. "The birth of a brand-new volcano in Hawaii? You think we're *causing* all that?"

"It's just strange that when all this stuff happens, you're all right there," he said. "There's a story here, I just know it. For God's sake, some guy was photographed walking through an active volcano at Volcanoes National Park right before the new island was born."

Rufus raised his hand. "That was me."

Allen stared at him. "Really?"

"Yeah, really. My sneakers melted. Want to see?"

Annie looked at him, surprised. "You kept them?"

"Well, we haven't actually stopped moving since then," he said defensively.

I said to Allen, "So what you're saying is you've been stalking us."

"No!"

"And doing a lousy job," Collum said. "He missed Colorado."

"Aw, cut him some slack," said Rufus. "We were there for barely a day."

Allen cried, "I just want to know what's going on, that's all!"

Gail said, "How did you get here tonight?"

"I took an Uber!" he shouted.

"Yeah, but…" Rufus said, then lapsed into silence as he shot us a look. We didn't need mind speech to know what he was thinking: *How much do we want to share with this guy?*

I sighed. "Well, we can't kick him out – he may never make it home."

"Huh?" Allen said, eyes bulging.

"Let's all get some sleep," I said. "We can figure everything out in the morning."

"Well, now," Collum said philosophically, "we may not figure it out even then. But at least we'll have had some sleep."

"Sounds good," Gail said as she stood up. "Are you assigning bedrooms, Raney?"

"Nope." I took a breath and stood. "So this house has a total of six bedrooms and they're all through that doorway." I pointed it out. "The master suite is all the way down on the left and it's taken. Mam's using the first room on the left. The rest are up for grabs. Pick whichever room suits you and your, uh, bunkmates." I laced my fingers through Collum's and stood. "Good night, everybody." And I pulled my favorite gnome behind me down the hall, confident they were all adults and could sort themselves out. Even Allen Owings.

Collum stopped just inside the doorway to my suite and whistled low. "Nice," he said. "Now I'm embarrassed I showed you my old room at my parents'."

"I did tell you my bed was bigger," I said, wrapping my arms around his neck and pulling him close. "But that's not the best part."

He kissed me, then rubbed his nose against mine. "Is this the best part?"

I undid his belt buckle. "Nope."

He helped me out of my shirt and bra. "This?"

"Mmm," I said. "Nope." I proceeded to help him out of his shirt as he slid my jeans down around my ankles.

"This?" he murmured as we embraced.

"Closer," I breathed. "But still nope." I walked out of my jeans and toward a door in the opposite wall, bringing him with me.

The rest of our clothing was shed pretty quickly. Amid the panting that followed, he said in my ear, "Closer…"

I felt for the doorknob behind my back and turned it, dancing him inward with the door. "Almost," I breathed. I peeked out to make sure the coast was clear. Then I drew him to the pool. "This, right here, is the best part." And I dove in.

Home! my nerve endings sang. *Homehomehomehomehome!*

Somehow, I kept it together long enough to make love with him. Then I relaxed and went to pieces, trusting that my dearest gnome would wait for me.

CHAPTER 7 – WEDNESDAY AT DAWN'S FIRST LIGHT

I wouldn't say we had a restful sleep, but it was restorative.

Until I awoke at dawn, filled with dread. The events of the previous day rushed back, and I knew today wouldn't be any better. I thought seriously about getting back in the pool and hiding there 'til it was all over.

Alas, I had a houseful of guests, and I couldn't leave the kitchen undefended while Rufus was under my roof. So I got up, showered, and got dressed. Then I made a pot of coffee and took my mug out onto the deck.

It was a typical fall morning in this world – chilly and too foggy to see the ocean. But I could hear the waves hitting the beach, and that was good enough for me.

Presently, Mam joined me, steaming mug in hand. "How'd you sleep?" I asked her.

"Not too well," she admitted. "Helen snores."

I gave her a wide-eyed smile. "Oh? I was kind of hoping it would be like that."

"So was she." Mam smiled back over the rim of her cup. Then she lowered it. "And you? Sweet dreams with your gnome?"

"Eventually," I admitted.

"I heard you two out here last night."

Heat rushed to my face. "Whoops. Sorry, Mam."

She waved it away. "You're a grown woman, Raney. I trust you to do what's best for you. You've certainly chosen better than I did." She looked away, out over the sea of clouds.

"I hope so. But who knows?" I said. "This is all still so new. We've known each other less than two months."

"I think he's a keeper," she said.

I grinned. "I think so, too." My smile faded. "We'll see, once life gets back to normal." I paused. "You don't think anyone else heard us, do you?"

"Rufus and Annie were busy," she said with a sly look. "And the others were too far away."

I wiped my brow dramatically, which made her chuckle. Then I sobered and voiced a fear I'd been trying hard to keep at bay. "I hope I can keep this place." If my career really was in the toilet, there was no way I'd be able to make the mortgage payments.

"Don't talk like that," Mam said. "Things have a way of working out."

Sure thing. All we have to do is survive the next few days. Weeks. However long it takes.

Piece of cake.

My early-morning respite was lovely, but it didn't last long enough. One by one, the team appeared (including Annie with Rufus) and the coffee disappeared. Collum made another pot, which was a good thing as his parents came out next, followed by Auntie Helen.

Allen Owings showed up last, consternation emanating from every pore. "I've been trying for half an hour to call my bureau chief, but there's no signal here. What's your wi-fi code?"

"So about that," I said. "Somebody want to explain it to him? I'm starting the eggs." Lucky for all of us, Mam had laid in a supply of provisions before the house did its thing.

"I'll help you, Raney," said Collum immediately.

"Fine," Gail said. "Rufus, come with me. Allen, have a seat." And in no-nonsense terms, Gail filled in the boy reporter, with a little help from Rufus. By the time the food was ready, Allen looked a little green.

"So we're not actually in Malibu?" he said faintly.

"No, we're in Malibu," I said. "Just not the one you're thinking of."

"Actually, it may not be called Malibu here," Rufus said. "We don't know that for sure."

50

"Stop confusing him," Gail said sharply. And to be honest, Allen looked he'd taken in about all he could manage.

"So how do I get a message to my boss?" he asked. "I need to check in."

"We need to find out what's going on in our world, too," Collum said. "We'll send a scout and you can go with them. After breakfast." He put plates and silverware on the breakfast bar. "Dig in, everybody."

As the cook, I was last in the serving line, but there were some eggs and bacon left for me – which was kind of momentous, considering Rufus had already been through twice. As I settled on the floor at the far end of the living room, I said to Allen, "Tell me again how you got here."

"I took an Uber," he said.

"After you got out of the Uber," I amended.

"Oh." He chewed for a minute. "It did seem a little weird, now that you mention it. I got out on Broad Beach Road and started walking toward the security perimeter. I could see it up ahead. But when I got close…" He shook his head. "I guess I got disoriented somehow. It was really dark, like the power had gone out. The only thing I could see was a glow from below the cliff, so I made for it, and it turned out to be your house. So I knocked on the door."

"So the gate was before you got to the perimeter?" Collum pressed.

"Yeah. It must have been."

I exchanged a guilty glance with my teammates. The gate we had used was outside the security perimeter. "I'm sure I closed it," Collum said.

"It looked sealed to me," Gail said.

We stared at each other for a moment. Then I called, "Tiger!"

She sounded annoyed. *I'm not answering any questions until I get fed.*

"I put out food for you," said Collum to the air.

It was gross. I'm not eating it. Where's my shrimp?

"No shrimp until you talk to us," I said. I wasn't sure I had any shrimp, to be honest, but I knew Mam had bought canned tuna – I'd seen it in the pantry when I was pulling breakfast together.

All right, fine, she grumbled, and waddled into the living room from the doorway to the hall. She sat down on her haunches and fixed her unblinking stare on me. *What?*

"Did you make a gate outside the security perimeter last night?"

Of course I did. How else was I supposed to bring all these people here?

"Fair enough. Did you maybe leave it open?"

My gates close on their own. She licked a paw and began grooming her ear with it.

"How long does that usually take?" Gail asked.

"I can't hear anything. Can you all hear him?" Allen asked, confused.

"It's a her," I said. I briefly considered telling her to let Allen hear her, but I knew it would be a waste of time. Instead, I repeated Gail's question. "Tiger, how long does it take for one of your gates to close?"

How should I know? I can't tell time. She began washing her other ear.

"Would it be closed before the next time you're fed?" Collum asked.

Oh, sure. A long time before.

"But you can't tell us in minutes or hours," I said.

Nope. Can I have my shrimp now?

I got up and headed for the kitchen, taking my dirty dishes with me. Tiger dashed in front of me, then slowed to a crawl.

"Are you *trying* to trip me?" I said.

Just making sure you keep on task.

I rolled my eyes and veered off toward the pantry. Luckily, there was a can of cocktail shrimp – the teeny-tiny ones you put in salads – way in the back. I opened that for her, hoping it would meet with her approval.

"That's the most logical explanation," Rufus said. "We'd only gotten back about an hour before he showed up."

"I'm a little concerned about what else might have gotten through that open gate," Gail said.

"Like animals?" Rufus asked. "Wildlife or something?"

"Or something," she said.

It must have been the way she said it that made me look out the kitchen window. I screamed.

"What?" Collum said.

"You guys, there's a golem out there!"

Gail looked out the windows onto the pool deck. "More than one."

"What's a golem?" Allen asked, and was ignored.

Rufus made for the closest bedroom. "I see several on this side of the house."

Collum had already checked the windows on the final side. "I believe we're surrounded," he said.

"Okay," I said. "What's our plan of attack?"

Gail looked out again. Then looked harder. Then turned to us. "They're gone."

We checked all around the house. *Poof!* No more golems.

"The house phased," Collum said. "The earth sensed the threat."

"Now you see 'em, now you don't," Rufus said as he rejoined the group in the living room.

This shrimp is weird, Tiger said.

"It's the only kind I've got," I said sharply. "Just eat it." My panic was still subsiding – I wasn't in the mood for her complaints.

She looked at me for a moment in surprise. Then she bent to her bowl and began chowing down.

I left her to it and returned to my spot on the living room floor. "They'll try again," I said. "Surgat must know by now that the house is protecting us."

"It will take them a long, long time to get through all of the alternatives," Niall said.

"Yeah, but they could get lucky," Collum said.

Mam got up and began collecting the used dishes. Annie joined her. But my thoughts – my fear – kept me rooted to the floor. I just kept thinking about the thing that tethered the house to our world. "What if they followed our electrical connection? Could they do that?"

Niall and Collum exchanged a glance. "Perhaps," Niall said, after a few moments.

"So what would happen if we cut the wire?" I pressed.

"We'd lose power here," Mam said as she loaded the dishwasher.

"Is the risk worth keeping the lights on?" I asked. "And remember it's not just us in this, you guys – we have others to worry about." I looked at Collum's parents and at Annie.

"We're not without our own resources, Raney," Niall reminded me, even as Kate took his hand.

"You're not," Collum said, "but Annie and Auntie Helen don't have your advantages."

"Don't be so sure," Auntie Helen said.

Rufus's head whipped around. "Something you'd like to share with us, Auntie?"

She smiled mysteriously. "Not yet."

"Mom?" asked Annie, as surprised as the rest of us. But Auntie Helen stayed mum.

After a moment, Gail said, "Sounds like the bad guys don't know who they're messing with." She crossed her arms and strode back to our group. "Okay. We need to go topside, the sooner the better. Initially I was thinking the non-combatants would be safest here, but now I think that would pose a bigger risk." She looked intently at Niall and Auntie Helen. "We may need you."

"Understood," Niall said. Auntie hadn't stopped smiling.

"All right," said Gail. "Let's move out."

"Just let me put my shoes on," my mother said as she headed for her room.

Surprised and scared, I stepped in front of her. "Mam?"

"Yes, my dear?"

"Damien's going to be there. You know that, right?"

I expected that to dent her serenity, but I was wrong. "Yes, I know."

My fear edged toward hysteria. "But what if he tries to grab you or something?" *What if I lose you? I can't lose you!*

"Dear Raney," she said, and embraced me. "Dear child. I've hidden from him for so long." She pulled away and looked into my eyes. "I'm too old for that now. Too old to run. Too old to hide. And I see what this has done to you."

"To me?"

"Yes, to you." She stroked my hair. "You've lived in the shadow of my fear for far too long. I need to resolve this."

I clutched at her and sobbed. *Can't lose you...*

She patted my back two or three times, then disengaged and went into her room. I watched her go, wiping my eyes. I hoped I would be as brave as her someday.

In a minute, she returned. She took my hand and smiled.

I turned toward the others. "Okay, we're ready. Let's go. I'll lock the door."

One more surprise awaited us.

Gail reached the top of the driveway first. There, she halted.

It took another few moments for Mam and me to reach her position. Once we got there, I could see why she'd stopped. There, in the middle of what would be Seaview Lane in my world, stood Cassius Kimball. The Aether. The man who had made Collum, Rufus, Gail and me into a team.

His eyes were still as black and unfathomable as ever.

He smiled at us. "All here? Good. You have done well, Elementals. In fact you have exceeded expectations, and for that we offer our thanks. But there is one more task we require of you before we release you.

"Come. It is time."

He raised his arms to the sky and brought them down – and dropped us into a hellscape.

CHAPTER 8 – WEDNESDAY, BACK HOME

In the universe where we'd slept, the sun was rising and the fog over the ocean had begun to dissipate. In this world – our real world – the sunrise was obscured by fire on the hillsides, and the haze over the ocean was not fog, but smoke.

Surgat must have awakened the golems early, for they had clearly been at work for some time. The flames marched ever closer to my neighborhood. I could see the lumbering creatures crossing the hillsides and marching down into the canyons. The human firefighters were doing their best, and every now and then they would manage to beat back the flames in one place – only to have a golem move back in and fire it up again.

The noise level was unbelievable – the roar of the fire, the shouts of the emergency personnel, the *whirr* of helicopters coming in with massive buckets of ocean water to douse as much of the fire as they could.

I looked back at my house. It was visible here in this reality, but its outline seemed to waver – whether due to the smoke or due to it phasing in and out, I couldn't be sure.

"Where did Cassius go?" Gail shouted in my ear.

I scanned the crowd. She was right – Cassius was gone. "I didn't see him leave," I shouted back. "Did he come with us?"

"I don't know!"

"Well, get up there and see what you can see!"

She looked as if I'd slapped her.

"Sorry," I said. "I didn't mean to order you…"

Impatiently, she waved off my apology. "You're right. I should have thought of it." And she was gone.

New shouts echoed from the hillsides. I could see why: Giant earth berms were springing up to surround the neighborhood. It was almost as if the Earth had responded to the need on her own.

Earth? Sure enough, Collum and his father were working together to raise the berms. They stood apart from the rest of the group, their eyes closed, their feet rooted to the earth. I had no doubt they were manipulating the native soil and rock the same way Collum had in Twin Lakes. Was that only yesterday?

And now I saw something else darting in and out amongst the golems – Rufus, with terrifying speed, was attacking each one in turn, pulling out its flaming heart and moving on to the next before the first had fully collapsed.

As brave an effort as he was making, I knew we couldn't win that way. There were too many of the creatures, and they had some way of communicating. Right now, Rufus had the element of surprise – but pretty soon he would meet one that would know he was coming.

Water would put out the fires, and I had a whole ocean at my back. The problem was getting enough of it where it needed to go without washing away the homes we were trying to save. A tsunami would bring the volume of water we'd need, but it would likely take houses back out to sea with it.

Then I remembered a trick I'd learned in Ireland.

"Mam!" I cried. "Can you reach any other undines?"

"I can try!"

I gave her a thumbs-up. "I'm going out over the ocean," I yelled.

Her eyes flew open wide. "What do you mean?"

I waved off her questions. "Have the others feed me water," I said.

"*What?*"

But I'd already begun to dissipate into a happy little cloud. It was harder here than it had been in Kilkenny – the air was very dry – but it got easier as I drifted out over the Pacific. There, I began to pull moisture to me, compacting and condensing until I had become a cloud of quite a respectable size.

I needed to be bigger, though, to douse the golems' fire. I looked around – and there below me, I saw what I'd hoped to see: undines and merpeople of every size and description were surfacing along the beach. They began vaporizing ocean water and sending it up to me – first a trickle, then a fire hose.

When I'd sopped up as much as I could handle, I began to move inland, toward the fire. But my movements were so sluggish and the weight of the water was so great that I was afraid I'd give way before I got to my target.

But Gail was beside me, under and behind me, and she stirred up the air currents to push me into place.

I was worried about Rufus, but I needn't have – Gail left me long enough to whisper a warning in his ear. I saw him glance up at me, then scurry away, out of the danger zone.

As soon as he was gone, I let loose.

I truly earned my nickname, the Torrent, that day. The rain came down so hard and fast that the fire was doused on the spot, and all the golems were swept away by the resulting flood. I was lucky – Collum and Niall saw the danger in time, and routed the floodwaters where they could do the least damage. In just a few minutes, it was over – the fire was out and the golems had been washed out to sea.

I came back to myself on the beach below my house. Gail found me and helped me dress – my clothes had fallen where I'd vaporized – and then carried, or flew, me back up the cliff to the house. There, I rejoined my teammates. Collum looked as tired as I felt, and Rufus's hair and eyebrows were singed – but we were thrilled to have won the battle. We exchanged high-fives as our friends and family cheered.

Suddenly, Allen Owings was at my elbow. I groaned inwardly. I had hoped he'd turn tail and run, the was he did the day we met the land wight at Lost Falls. Oh haha, no.

"That was amazing!"

"Thanks, Allen."

"Can I ask you some questions?"

"Um…"

"How is it that your friend isn't burned to a crisp? And did you really turn into a *cloud*? How does that work, exactly?"

"It's a trick I learned in Ireland," I said. Which was true, as far as it went.

"But is it *magic*, or what?"

"Kind of? I guess you could say it's Water magic, with a dollop of Air magic."

I'd found, as a celebrity, that sometimes the smartest thing to do was to tell the truth, because it often provided the most confusing answer. It definitely worked this time. I could almost hear the cogs of Allen's brain creaking as he tried to make sense of what I'd just said. "But…"

"Listen, can we talk later? I'm pretty sure this isn't over."

"It's not?"

In response, I gave him a happy little shrug and walked away.

Unfortunately for us, I was right – it wasn't over. As I rejoined my teammates and our cheering section, I noticed Rufus wasn't smiling. "What's up?" I asked him.

He nodded grimly toward the ridge where the land dropped off toward the beach. "Them," he said.

I ran toward the edge, but I didn't have to get close to see what he was talking about. The golems were back. They were marching out of the surf and swarming up our side of the canyon – and as they came on, I could see they weren't built exactly like the golems we'd run into before. These each had one arm that ended in a tube or nozzle, and they were using these built-in flamethrowers to reignite the hills.

Rufus had followed me, and now Collum and Gail joined us. "They won't get much traction," I said. "The ground's soaked."

"There are so many of them," Annie said in dismay. She looked up at Rufus, who put an arm around her.

"They're shiny," Collum said suddenly.

I cocked an eyebrow. "You like them that much?"

He rolled his eyes. "No, not that kind of shiny. The ones we ran into before were definitely made of clay. It was easy to break off pieces of them. Right?"

"Right," I said. "Like Play-Doh."

"I don't think these are like Play-Doh," Collum said. "I think they're tempered."

"Or fired in a kiln," Gail said. She tore her eyes away from the sight to focus on us. "Okay. Either they've adapted or they've been adapted. Doesn't matter. The point is we won't be able to take them down the way we have in the past. Options?"

"Fired clay is hard," Collum said, "but it can also crack. We could break them with something heavy. Or drop something on them from the air."

"Or both," Gail said. "I can't lift anything too heavy, but the higher I go, the faster it will be going when it hits."

Our attention was caught by a couple of county deputies who were thinking along the same lines as we were. "Stop right there!" one of them shouted, pointing a firearm at the closest golem. The brainless golem, of course, kept coming. So the deputy shot him.

The bullet pinged off the creature's forehead.

More shots. More ricocheting bullets.

"So clearly, breaking them isn't going to work," Rufus said. "Any other ideas?"

Collum had already stepped forward. He opened a deep trench in the earth in front of the creatures, and sure enough, they walked up to it and fell right in. When the trench was full of about twenty golems, he snapped it shut. Then he began to set up another trench.

"Collum!" I yelled, my eyes on the first trench. A hand was clawing its way up out of the dirt. Then another. And another.

"They're like goddamned zombies!" Rufus said, revving up his internal fire to do battle with them.

"Wait!" I said. "You can't fight fire with fire!"

"This is no time for platitudes, Raney!" Rufus yelled back.

I glared at him. "You fight fire with *ice*," I said.

"Clever girl," said a voice behind me. I turned to see Gail's former colleague Ben Gelber joining us at last. He looked the same as he had on Skype – close-cropped gray hair and a not-too-prominent nose. He wore a threadbare blue cardigan over a white polo shirt, but no yarmulke. I noticed he and Gail were more or less the same height.

"It's about time you got here," Gail growled.

"I was detained," he said mildly.

"Well, that's just great," she said. "Now that you're here, how about giving us some help? Have you ever seen a golem behave this way? And how do we stop them?"

He shook his head, chuckling. "There's no precedent in the literature for what these creatures are doing. Or none that I'm aware of, at least." He nodded toward me. "I think your undine's idea is worth a try, though. If you've tried everything else, maybe freezing them will do the trick. If nothing else, it could make them brittle enough to shatter."

"How do we do it, though?" I said. "The only being I've seen that can create freezing conditions is…" I looked at Gail. "You think you could find her?"

She snorted. "That sprite was more trouble than she was worth." Her smile turned crafty. "But the sylph owes me one. Be right back." And she swirled away.

"Hurry!" I yelled after her. Then I turned back to the advancing golems. My favorite gnome was still building trenches, which were slowing them down, at least. But still more rose from the sea – way more than the floods had ever washed away.

61

"Where are they all *coming* from?" Rufus said. "And where the hell is Damien? If we found him, we could take him down. That would distract Surgat from making more of these damn things."

I could tell Collum was getting tired. He'd been moving a lot of earth – and even though he wasn't lifting a shovel, it was still backbreaking work. "There must be an access point – a gate – just offshore. I'm going to see if I can find it and seal it somehow." And I began to run toward the beach.

My route took me past a line of golems, but my presence didn't seem to bother them. They didn't see me as a threat, I guess. Although come to think of it, they hadn't attacked any of us – not even Rufus when he was taking them out. I'd been sure they would turn on him, but they never had.

We weren't their targets. They had a different mission: setting fires and keeping them going.

The hills needed to be ablaze for some reason.

Why did that sound familiar?

I shook my head. It would come to me eventually. Then I waded into the sea.

I noted the spot where the golems were surfacing and paused. Dissolved, I could pass through the gate undetected – but if there were no water on the other end, I'd have zero control over the timing of my reassembly. Plus I'd be soaking wet and naked. Swimming down to the gate seemed like a better idea.

I stretched out my arms and linked my hands to surface dive – and something barreled into me from behind.

I faceplanted into the water and rolled over, spluttering. "Seriously?" I yelled at my attacker.

Just a few yards away, a pudgy orange tabby cat was doing a pretty good dog paddle. *Don't go down there! It won't help!*

"Oh, really? And what will?" I sneered. Then I sneezed water out of my nostrils and glared at her.

Look, sister. I'm trying to help you. Have I steered you wrong yet?

"There's a first time for everything," I muttered. She was right, but I was mad at her.

With more patience than I'd ever seen her exhibit, she paddled in a circle until she was facing my house. We had a really good view of it from here, silhouetted against the flames. *Look*, she said. *What's different?*

"I don't have time for guessing games," I snarled. But then I took a good look, and another. The house had been fading in and out before, but slowly. Now the cycle had accelerated. "It looks like a motor revving up," I said. Then I looked at Tiger in alarm. "Damien's tapping the electrical connection!"

I didn't have to follow the golems to their source. I just needed to cut their power source. It meant losing the connection to my house in the other universe, but the Earth should be able to bring it back here when the coast was clear. I hoped.

"Go tell the guys," I told the cat. "I'll go up there and figure out where the cutoff switch is."

It'll take you too long to climb those stairs. Follow me. She winked out.

I shrugged and followed her.

In a moment, we were just outside the front door. The house was blinking rapidly now, like a freeze-frame cartoon. "Close the gate!" I yelled. "There are golems on the other side of it!"

She grumbled but complied. Then she slipped out through a new gate to find one of the guys. Which was excellent, because I had no idea where to look for the main shut-off switch. I very much hoped it wasn't inside the house.

Tiger returned with Rufus. Apparently she'd briefed him on the way, because he said, "Where's your breaker box?"

I shrugged expressively.

"Right," he said. "Okay. Where's your electric meter?"

"My what?"

"Funny-shaped device with spinning dials. Some of them spin faster than others."

"Oh!" I said. "It's by the garage." Which, thank God, was not connected to the house, or it would have been phasing in and out, too. I led him to the spot and stared hard at the thing; all the dials were spinning. "My next electric bill is gonna be killer, isn't it?"

"All the more reason to cut off the juice right now," he said with a grin, and crouched to inspect the device. He looked up at me. "If we were following protocol, I would have you call the power company to come out here and shut it off for us. But we don't have that kind of time."

The dials were behind a cylindrical glass faceplate and a metal retaining ring. He grabbed a wire loop with a tag that was threaded through a connector on the retaining ring, pinched it between a thumb and forefinger, and heated it until it fell apart. I smelled hot metal.

The ring slid right off. Then he placed his hands on the glass bowl and started rocking it up and down. "By rights," he said as he worked, "I should be wearing rubber gloves and boots. And I should have already killed the main circuit breaker."

"Why?"

"Because the wires are hot. Electrified. Could start a fire, or it could fry me." He grinned. "Assuming I was a hundred percent human, which I'm not." He grunted, then pulled the glass cover and the meter free and set it on the ground. "Now those leads in there are hot," he told me, pointing. "Don't touch them."

"Yes, sir," I said with a little salute. Then I turned and sucked in a breath. My house was gone.

I knew it was likely to happen when we shut off the power. I just didn't realize how it would make me feel.

Homeless. I felt homeless. Like I'd lost everything.

"Raney?"

"My house," I said. Tears streamed down my face.

"Aww." He put a hand on my shoulder. "You'll get it back. You know that, right?"

"Yeah, I know, but..." I snuffled. "It's just so..." I shook my head.

"At least the golems have stopped coming," he said.

I looked out to the spot where they'd been lumbering up out of the water. He was right – the last of the golems trudged ashore. "We got that much done, at least," I said.

"Yay for us. Right?"

"Right." But then I took a better look at the scene before us. "Rufus?"

"Yeah?"

"Remember that drawing in Auntie's book? The one that shows the gate to the big, bad Door?"

"Kind of. Why?"

I pulled my phone out of my jeans pocket and flipped rapidly through the photos until I found what I was looking for: the photos I'd taken of the pages in the book the original Fire Key guardians had given Auntie. I stopped at the one of the scene with the fiery portal. I'd told Gail the view didn't look familiar to me.

I passed the phone to Rufus, who glanced at the photo and then at the scene before us. "Oh," he said. "Oh, shit."

It was easy to see the resemblance, now that the house was out of the way. There was the burning vegetation along the crest of the rise on the right. There, below, was the rocky beach. The only thing missing – other than the mouth of hell – was the waterspout.

And then, right on cue, the waterspout appeared.

A moment later, Windy breezed in. She wore a look of triumph that turned immediately to dismay. "What?" she said. "I couldn't find Anemone – she's nowhere near Mount Elbert. So I came back here and made a plan B. In case you didn't have any luck with stopping the golems at their source, I planned to position the waterspout over the gate." Then she looked around. "Where's the house?"

"Oh, dear," said Auntie from behind us. I turned around. Tiger had brought everyone – even Collum, fresh from making the last zombie golem pit. He approached me, shoulders slumped in defeat.

I rubbed his back. "It's okay," I said with mock cheerfulness. "It gets worse."

We had a killer view from the vantage point of my garage. While Rufus passed my phone around, Auntie stepped out in front of all of us. "Oh, dear," she said again. "It's exactly like the book."

"Yep," I said.

"Oh," Gail said faintly. "Oh, shit."

CHAPTER 9 – WEDNESDAY, WHEN A NEW DOOR OPENED

While we all stood there in shock, things were happening below us. Dreadful things.

A line of flame shot out from the canyon across the ocean. "Water doesn't burn," I said in disbelief.

"Neither does Air," Gail said. But the air near the surface of the water seemed to catch fire and burn open a hole there. No, not a hole – a portal.

"Nor does Earth," said Collum. But the fire somehow reached the sand below the waves and set it afire, too.

"There's only one Element missing," Mam said. "Aether."

I shook my head. "I think it's covered."

Fire rimmed the portal. Beyond the flaming opening, I couldn't see anything – the interior was black as night.

We exchanged glances, unsure of what to do. The moment stretched.

Humans, Tiger finally said in disgust. She lumbered to the edge of the cliff and jumped.

"Tiger, no!" I cried. I had visions of all those cat videos I'd seen on social media – the ones where the kitty appears to be calculating the square root of an imaginary number or something, and then jumps for the top of a door and misses.

Tiger didn't miss, though. Somehow she sailed, legs stretched out like a superhero, and landed in the center of the flaming portal.

She turned toward us and sat, then stared at us without blinking. *Are you coming or not?*

I looked around. The fires on the hillsides were burning themselves out. The shiny golems were trooping back to their den beneath the waves. The waterspout was still churning offshore, but appeared to be losing its punch.

And my house was still gone.

"This whole thing was staged to open the portal," Collum said in disgust.

"And Surgat knew exactly what to do, too," Gail said. "That demon knows more than he's been letting on."

Rufus looked at her. "Got the Air Key?"

She patted her left hip where a small lump stuck out. Somewhere along the way – maybe when she went to find Anemone – she had traded her usual diaphanous style for a black-and-white Lycra ensemble. I wished I had one. I was still wearing the jeans and team t-shirt I'd donned before we tackled Mount Elbert. So were Collum and Rufus, I noticed.

"Suit up," Collum said, tossing Gail her t-shirt. He turned to the others – his parents, my mother, Annie and Auntie Helen, and Ben Gelber – and said, "We'll be back as soon as we can."

"Oh, no, me boyo," Kate Barth said, hands on her hips. "Sure and you're not leaving *us* behind."

"But Mam," he said, "it'll be dangerous."

"And hasn't it been dangerous all these years, with himself in charge of guarding the Earth Key," she returned, her eyes flashing toward her husband. "We'll see this through with you, see if we don't." Then her voice softened. "We won't be a bother."

"And you may need another hand," Niall said.

Collum raised his arms in defeat.

"We're coming, too," Annie said stoutly. "Auntie Helen says you'll need her, and…" She paused, then flung her arms around Rufus. "I can't lose you."

Rufus returned the embrace.

Can't lose you… I looked at Mam. "I can't talk you out of this, can I?"

Her expression mirrored mine – fear, longing, determination, and love. "No," was all she said.

I hugged her fiercely, then stepped back and knuckled tears from my eyes. "Look at us," I said, my voice breaking. "A couple of silly undines getting all worked up."

"Yeah," she said, laughing and crying at the same time.

I kissed her cheek. Then I looked at the mouth of hell and the cat seated before it. "Hey, Tiger," I called. "How do we do this? Just step off the edge?"

She regarded me silently, as if the answer were so obvious that she couldn't be bothered to answer.

"Okay, but if I break my neck, I'm blaming you," I said, and took Mam's hand.

You wouldn't break your neck anyway. You'd turn to water first. Which was accurate, but it didn't make me feel any more charitable toward her.

As I raised my foot to take the first step, I heard Ben Gelber say, "Just like old times, eh, Gail?"

Gail snorted. "Let's hope it's not *too* much like old times."

I shrieked as both feet slid out from under me. I sat down hard on nothing at all and rode – air currents, maybe? I couldn't tell – all the way to gate.

Mam was right behind me. Then came Auntie Helen, Rufus and Annie, Collum and his parents, and Ben. Gail skipped the ride and blew down in her usual way, materializing in a perfect three-point landing like a superhero.

I had to force myself not to roll my eyes. All four of us were superheroes, but she was the only one who felt the need to show off like that. I wondered if it was for Ben. I also wondered about their relationship and when it had gone sour. She'd been nothing but professional toward him when we spoke with him by Skype, and nothing but cranky since learning she'd have to see him in the flesh. And too, the animosity all seemed to be on her side – Ben seemed perfectly happy to be here with us, but Gail radiated resentment, as if she expected she'd have to babysit him.

I sure hoped we wouldn't have to babysit him. I suspected none of us would have time for it.

All of these thoughts zipped through my mind at once. I stowed them away carefully, for in-depth contemplation later. Right now, a big, black chasm yawned before us, and we had no choice but to enter it.

I mean, I guess we could have skipped out on the whole thing. But Cassius had said we had one more task to complete, and I was certain now that he hadn't meant corralling golems and putting out brush fires.

"Okay," Rufus said. "Who's going in first?"

"Tiger," I said, pointing. She had already started through the portal. All I could see of her was her hind legs and tail, and in a moment, those too had disappeared. The very tip of her tail was the last thing to go. I took a deep breath and stepped forward.

But Rufus strong-armed me. "My turn," he said. "Fire is my Element, after all."

"Oh, like Air was mine," I scoffed, "and I still went first up top."

Eyes alight with humor, he put his thumb to his nose and wiggled his fingers at me. Then he was gone. Annie rushed after him.

With a wink at us, Auntie Helen followed them.

Kate looked nervous. "Will the gate stay open for our return, do you think, Niall?"

"Doubtful," he said. "Come on, love." And they walked through together.

That left Collum, Mam, and me. My brave gnome took my hand in one of his, and my mother's hand in the other. Then the three of us crossed together.

This crossing was different from any other gate into the Otherworld I'd used so far. Normally there's a moment of nothing, and then you're through. It's like stepping through a veil, in a way, with the world on one side feeling very much like the one on the other.

This time, though, the *nothing* had a different quality. It felt cold and still. And the world on the other side had that same cold, still quality.

Nothing moved – there was neither wind nor waves. We stood in shin-deep water the color of steel, a few yards from an ashen shingle. The sky above was a sullen gray. The flames ringing the fast-closing portal behind us were a pale imitation of the ones in our world.

We were the most colorful things in this colorless world.

There was movement in front of us. Someone on the beach was waving – a man who appeared to be my age, bearded, and wearing a technical hoodie and jeans. After a moment, a little girl joined him. The man picked her up and settled her on his hip. Then they both waved at us, motioning us to move faster to join them.

I was just thinking that there was something about the man that seemed familiar when Collum slowed to a stop. "Conor?" he said.

"Conor!" Kate cried at virtually the same time. "Dora!" She let go of her husband's hand and ran, her feet kicking up the gray water. "Oh, my children! Oh, my heart!" She was sobbing as she reached them. Conor hugged her and handed over the child, and she hugged them both.

Niall arrived and held them all, laughing in disbelief.

Collum stood beside me, still clinging to my hand. "Go on," I said gently.

He shook his head. "This can't be. It's a trick. It has to be." His voice rose. "You're dead!"

Conor disentangled himself from his parents and took a few steps toward us, staying clear of the water's edge. He was built like his mother – taller and thinner than Collum. "It's no trick," he called. "Or rather, the trick is on Dora and me. You see, this is the Underworld. The land of the dead." He shook his head, amazed. "Believe me, Collum, I'm as shocked to see you and Mam and Da as you are to see me."

At last, Collum stumbled forward. "It's really you," he said in wonder. "It's really you." And with a sob, my formerly stoic gnome fell into his brother's arms.

The rest of us took our time in reaching the shore. The others stood in a group to one side, shifting uncomfortably. A sobbing gnome was a lot to take in on the best of days, and here we were confronted with four of them, plus Kate. Then, too, I'm sure the others were wondering who among their own beloved dead they might run into here. The thought had certainly crossed my mind, although I couldn't think of anyone who fit the bill – all of Mam's relations were still living, as far as I knew, and Damien's description of his parents hadn't instilled in me any desire to meet them.

The thought of Damien reminded me of why we were here. We were supposed to be looking for the Door with the locks into which the four Elemental Keys fit. Surely it couldn't be in the land of the dead, could it?

Conor seemed most likely to have answers, if anyone here had them. Warily, I approached the brothers.

Conor spotted me and pulled out of Collum's bear hug. "Hi," he said. "You look familiar. Have we met?"

Well, yeah, but you were a corpse at the time…

Collum rescued me. "This is Raney Meadows. She's an actress. *Story of a Homicide?*"

Daylight dawned. "Oh, the TV show! Sure. It's one of my favorites." He frowned and looked away. "Well, it was." Then he took in the two of us. "So wait – how did you two meet?"

"Um, well, I was through-hiking the A.T. when I sort of…" *Stumbled across your corpse.* I threw Collum a panicked look.

"She helped me track down your killer," he filled in. Then his lips quirked up at one corner. "Wow. That's a thing I never thought I'd say."

Conor's face closed like a fist. "Alex Drake," he said. "Was he brought to justice?"

"In a manner of speaking," I said. "Cloch turned him over to Shenandoah and Potomac. The river goddesses," I explained.

"Cloch?" he said, eyes wide. "The land wight Cloch?"

"The very same," said Collum.

Conor cocked his head. "This sounds like quite a tale, bro."

"It is. But unfortunately, it will have to wait for another time. We're on a mission."

"We're looking for a Door that requires four Keys to open," I said. "One Key for each Element. Do you know anything about it? Have you heard of it?"

Conor's brow furrowed. "Isn't Da the guardian of one of those Keys?"

"He was," said Collum. "And thereby hangs another tale, sadder than the first."

Conor thought for a moment, then shook his head.

I thought of another angle. "Have you seen Damien Jones recently?"

An emotion I didn't recognize flared in Conor's eyes. It doesn't often happen that I can't place an emotion – it's kind of my thing, after all – but this one mystified me. Maybe it was because Conor was dead, I don't know. Anyway, he said evenly, "What's Damien Jones got to do with all this?"

"He's possessed by a demon," Collum said. "And the demon wants the Keys so he can open the Door." Which was a much better answer than I had been about to give – *he's my father* would not have helped the situation at all.

Conor made a sort of rolling motion with one hand,. "And behind the Door is...?"

"A Tool that could destroy the Earth."

"Ah. That's a good thing to prevent."

"We think so," said Collum, deadpan. "The Earth does, too. Raney and I – and Rufus and Gail over there – the four of us are tasked with stopping them."

"*That's* what's different about you," Conor said. "Your eyes used to be brown."

"Mine were marine blue," I said. "Now we all have hazel eyes. And a little bit of each other's powers, as well."

"Yours used to be brown, too," Collum said wistfully.

Conor smiled and looked down. "Yeah, well, a lot of things are different here." He looked up. "It's funny that you mention Damien Jones. I caught a glimpse of him not long ago."

"How long?" I asked instantly.

Conor's shrug was exactly like his brother's. "I'm not sure. Time moves differently here."

"Was it today?" Collum asked. "A few hours ago? A few minutes ago?"

"Not long ago," was the best Conor could do.

I was impatient with his answer, but I tried not to let it show. Instead, I tried a different tack. "Where was he?"

Conor's expression cleared. "I can show you," he said, and set off, up the beach. Collum motioned to the group to follow us. Dora came, too, skipping along between her parents.

Rufus and Gail made their way to us. "What's going on?" Gail asked.

"Conor's seen Damien. He can't tell us how recently, but he's going to show us where it was," I said.

We hiked a fair distance along the shingle. At a break between dunes, Conor turned inland. Beyond the line of low dunes was a landscape of scrubby brush. Everything was still shades of gray, but I had the distinct impression that Conor's hoodie – which had been neon green in real life – stood out like a beacon against the silvery gray of the plants.

It looked like we were heading toward a woodland. The trees had black-and-gray trunks, and their gray branches were leafed out in gray, mature leaves. "Is that where you live?" Kate asked.

Over his shoulder, Conor threw her a puzzled frown. "This is where we live, Mam. All of this." He stretched out his arms to encompass everything we could see.

"But do you have a house, is what I'm asking."

"It's not here," Dora said.

"Where is it?" Niall asked her.

She looked sad. "It's where you live."

Wordlessly, he picked her up and kissed her.

"Where are the other dead people?" Collum asked his brother.

"Not here, as you've noticed," said Conor. He turned around and walked backward while talked. "The land of the dead is a big place. We try to avoid one another if we can."

"Why?" asked Ben.

"And you are…?" Conor asked.

"Ben Gelber," he said. "I'm sort of a consultant to the team." Gail rolled her eyes but let it pass.

Conor nodded. "Pleased to meet you, Ben. So there are a lot of reasons why the dead would want to avoid one another. Some are in denial about their status as non-living beings, and seeing other spirits upsets them. Others have certain religious beliefs about heaven and Valhalla and the like – they tend to stay to themselves. You've heard the old joke about the Baptists in heaven?"

A few of the older folks chuckled. "I haven't," I said.

"Really?" Conor and Collum said together, then looked at each other and grinned.

Collum picked up the thread. "Okay. So this guy dies and St. Peter greets him at the Heavenly Gates. 'Let me show you around,' St. Peter says, and starts giving him a tour. They pass the Methodist heaven and the Lutheran heaven and everything's fine. Then St. Peter puts a finger to his lips and says, 'We have to be vey quiet as we pass this next group.'

"So they tiptoe past. And when they get clear, the new guy says, 'What was that all about?'

"And St. Peter says, 'They're Baptists. They think they're the only ones here.'"

Everyone laughed. Then Niall said, "In Ireland, it's the Catholics," and we all laughed again.

By this point, we'd reached the edge of the woods. "How much farther, dude?" Collum said.

"Not too far," said Conor.

"I don't like the woods," said Dora, and hid her face in her father's shirt collar.

"Why ever not?" Kate asked.

"It's scary." Dora reached for her mother, who took her from Niall's arms.

Conor stopped. "We don't all need to go. It's not like the man's still there. Some of you can wait here if you're tired – we'll swing back and pick you up."

"I want to stay here with Collum," Dora announced.

"I'm not staying," he told her. "Mam and Da will stay with you, if you don't want to go."

"No!" she cried, and squirmed to be let down. Then she ran to Collum and held her arms up.

I realized that while he'd greeted Conor, he had yet to interact with his sister. I thought maybe he'd refuse her, or continue to ignore her. But no. He sighed and picked her up. She nestled against his chest and stuck her thumb in her mouth.

"Minx," he said, nuzzling her hair. She giggled.

Conor watched them with a look of longing.

I remembered the family dynamic. After Dora's death, Kate had become very protective of Conor, leaving Collum to fend for himself. Collum was the eldest, but he was still just a kid. He couldn't very well hate his mother, so he ended up jealous of Conor, and the two boys grew up not getting along. They had only begun to work through those complicated feelings when Conor was killed.

I'd felt so sorry for Collum that I hadn't thought about what the dynamic had done to his brother – but now, here it was, right in front of me. Conor wanted what Dora had – the certainty that he could curl up against their brother's chest and be loved.

My emotional undine heart opened to him. I was about to cross the space between us and give him a hug when I heard what sounded like a motor running – except it wasn't a motor at all. Conor looked down and smiled. "Tiger," he said. "You came."

Of course. And she sprang up into his arms.

He nuzzled her fur and sighed happily. Then he looked up at us. "Everybody rested? All right. Let's go on." And he plunged into the woods, Tiger propped on his shoulder.

As we hiked along behind him, I noticed Dora watching me with dark, unfathomable eyes. Her thumb came out of her mouth with an audible *pop* and she asked Collum, "Who's that?"

"That's Raney," he said.

"Hi, Dora," I said. "It's nice to meet you."

The thumb went back in her mouth and she put her head back down. But she smiled at me. Up came her head again. "Is she nice?" she asked Collum.

"Very nice," he said.

"Thanks," I told him, and he grinned at me.

Then Dora reached for me. I'm not the most adept person with small children – I've had almost no practice – but what was I going to do, say no? So we made the transfer and my heart melted.

"You smell like the sea," she said.

"Yeah?" I ducked my chin to look into her face. "Is that good or bad?"

"Good," she said with a sigh. The thumb went back in and she closed her eyes.

Collum grinned at me. "You passed."

"I didn't know there was a test," I said, somewhat tartly. He laughed and gave me a sidearmed hug.

All at once, the trees thinned, and we were in a clearing. A lone tree stood in the center, as gray and unmoving as everything else around us. Mushrooms stood sentinel in a ring around the tree.

"You saw Damien here?" Rufus asked. "In a fairy ring?"

"Seems odd, doesn't it?" Conor said. "But yeah, that's where he was." He put Tiger down so she could sniff at the mushrooms.

"Where were you when you saw him?" Gail asked.

Conor gestured back the way we came. "When I spotted him, I sort of hid," he said. "It's not that common to see others here, and it's *really* uncommon to see a living person like yourselves." His expression darkened. "And I have a history with him."

I remembered that unreadable expression he'd worn earlier, the first time we mentioned his name. "Do tell," I said, shifting Dora in my arms. I wasn't accustomed to holding a child for this long, and one of my hands had gone to sleep.

Conor cut a glance toward the fairy ring. "Let's get away from here. There's no telling what might come through this thing."

"Sounds like a plan," Rufus said. "We've had our fill of the Good Neighbors over the past few weeks."

"Here, Raney, I've got her," Kate said, lifting Dora from my arms. She sighed and resumed sucking her thumb briefly as her mother resettled her.

"Thanks." I smiled and shook out my hand to try to make the pins-and-needles feeling go away faster. Then I rejoined the group as Conor put some distance between us and the fairy ring.

Chapter 10 – About that fairy ring, and more

Presently Conor stopped and faced us. "I think this is far enough. Y'know, in college, I learned that fairy rings aren't magic at all. It's a type of fungus that grows out from the center. The middle dies off eventually. That's what makes the ring shape." He barked a laugh. "That's what they told me, anyway. If only they knew the truth."

"Science can't explain everything," Ben said brightly. "Isn't that what they told us in the service, Gail? Science can't explain how you do what you do, so of course it can't be done."

She nodded. "But if you eliminate all the rational possibilities, magic is the only explanation. By definition."

"Exactly. But they weren't buying that at my school," Conor said with a sad smile.

"Anyway," said Collum, "about Damien."

"Right." He dropped into a crouch, forearms resting on his knees. "So. The last time I saw you was at the enchanted – I mean, at your house."

Collum grimaced. *The enchanted cottage* was Conor's unflattering nickname for the family cabin Collum had more or less inherited. "Right. It was our regular Wednesday night dinner. You told me Drake was planning to do something crazy and illegal, and you planned to stop him somehow."

"Yeah. That didn't go so well."

"Why didn't you come straight out and tell me he was going to destroy Lost Falls?"

Conor gazed up at him. "I wanted to protect you. I was afraid Drake would come after you if you knew too much."

"And then he did anyway."

"Not 'til we went after him," I corrected. "And anyway, you're the one who told him Conor was your brother."

"Yeah, well, you're the one who told Damien..." He snapped his mouth closed.

Conor looked between the two of us. "Told Damien what?"

Might as well lay all the cards on the table. "He's my father," I said. To Conor's look of consternation, I said, "Damien kidnapped my mother and impregnated her. I'm the result. I'd never met him until a few weeks ago."

I thought he'd reject me. Instead, he glanced at Gail and Rufus, and then back to Collum. "So you're all half-human?"

"Yes," Collum said. "Why?"

"It makes a difference, that's all," Conor said.

"Makes a difference in *what?*" Rufus said, moving closer to Conor. "Swear to God, if somebody doesn't start *explaining* stuff to us..."

Now Gail strode forward. She stopped halfway between Rufus and me, crossed her arms, and glared at Conor. Consciously or subconsciously, I struck the same pose. So did Rufus.

So did Collum. "Spill it, little brother," he said.

"Look, I'm not the right person..." he began.

"Nobody's the right person," Collum shot back, "except the Fair Folk, and they want some kind of unspecified *payment* for the information, which we're not in the mood to give them. So we've basically been flying blind for the past six weeks. So you just need to tell us what you know, right now."

"Please," I added. Collum stared at me incredulously. I shrugged. *Hey, it's worth a shot.*

Conor looked deflated. "Okay, okay. I'll tell you what I know about it. But I need to tell you about Damien first, because it's all one thing."

"Fine," Collum said.

"Fine," Conor repeated. He drew in a breath. "Okay. So that night, I couldn't sleep. Tossed and turned. In the middle of the night, I got up and copied everything onto a thumb drive and stuck it under my desk. Did you find it?"

"I did," I said. "Tiger told me where to look. Go on."

He smiled. "She's the best cat," he said. "Anyway, I thought making a copy of the data would help my anxiety, but it didn't. I finally got up really early the next morning. I fed Tiger, grabbed my laptop, and drove up to Alex Drake's office on Schoolhouse Ridge. I knew it was too early for his office staff to be there – I figured I would be able to walk in and confront him without having to run a gantlet of admin staff." He took a better look at Rufus. "Aren't you with the union? I learned that maneuver from you guys."

Rufus nodded but said nothing.

"Anyway," he resumed, "I was surprised to hear Drake having a meeting with someone so early. The sun was barely up, and here he was, deep in conversation in his office. I thought about coming back, but no – I needed to stop him. So I walked in. And there he was, meeting with Damien Jones." He cut a look at me. I was pretty sure it was involuntary.

"You knew who he was?" I asked.

Conor nodded. "I knew a guy in college who was obsessed with getting rich. In his spare time, he would look up billionaires and research their backgrounds to find out how they'd made their money. Jones was one of his favorites. The guy made his fortune by manufacturing toilet paper."

"I'd heard that," I said.

Conor shook his head. "My buddy thought it was a brilliant move. He'd say, 'Damien Jones built a recession-proof business. People will never stop buying toilet paper.'"

"Until we run out of trees," Gail said.

"They're a renewable resource, though. You just plant more," said Rufus.

"But it takes hundreds of years for them to grow back," she argued.

"Hemp grows faster and makes paper that's just as good," Collum said.

"Yeah, well, good luck getting it legalized," Gail said.

I broke in. "How about we let the guy finish his story?"

"Right," Collum said. "Sorry. Go on."

"I brought that tangent on myself, to be honest," Conor said ruefully. "Anyway, yes, I knew who Damien Jones was, and I recognized him as soon as I stepped into Drake's office. But he was different. Odd. I sensed another personality in the room."

"Surgat," I said. "That's the demon controlling him. He Who Opens All Locks."

He nodded thoughtfully. "That was probably it. Anyway, there I was, with both of them in the room. I'd heard rumors about big money backing the Lost Falls project, and as soon as I saw Jones, I put two and two together. So I went right into the speech I was going to give Drake." He looked up at the colorless sky beyond the colorless leaves. "I didn't get very far. Damien came at me and held me in a chokehold while Drake took my laptop and looked through it for the evidence I'd said I had. Except it wasn't there." He laughed shortly. "In my exhaustion the night before, instead of *copying* all the files onto the thumb drive, I'd *moved* them there."

"They could have let you go," Collum said quietly.

"Nah," Conor said. "They knew from what I'd already said that I knew what they were up to. So the two of them marched me out to the cliff above the river and…"

A scene flashed before my mind's eye: Three men standing high above the Shenandoah River, one of them struggling, one with demonic strength. A hand to the crown of the head, a fatal twist…

"Drake didn't kill you," I said. "Damien did."

His rock-solid gaze, so like his brother's, met mine. "Got it in one," he said.

And now I knew what that unreadable look of his had been: Loathing, behind a mask of gnomic stoicism.

Conor stood, finally. "So yeah, when I saw him materialize in the fairy ring, I hid. It's not like he could have killed me a second time, but I still wasn't interested in running into him again."

"Makes perfect sense," Collum said.

"I am so sorry," I said, walking toward him. "I hate him, too." Then I hugged him. A moment later, his arms came around me.

We stood like that for a little while, and then we were enveloped in other arms: Kate's, Niall's, Collum's, even Dora's. I tried to slip out of the pile of Barths, but it was no use. They were determined to comfort me, too.

We might have stayed like that forever, but Gail cleared her throat. "So about that Door," she said.

Conor groaned. "Right. The Door." He pulled away and the group hug fell apart. Even so, the Barths stayed near him. I backed off a few paces so I could see everyone. Gail and Rufus hadn't moved, although Annie was holding Rufus's hand. The two older women had taken seats on a fallen tree. Ben Gelber was the farthest away – he caught me looking at him and gave me a guilty smile.

Why guilty? Did he have to pee? Or was he trying to leave without anyone noticing?

And if he was trying to leave, where was he planning to go? As far as I knew, the gate we'd come through was closed, and the only other way out – that we knew of, anyway – was through the fairy ring. And I had no idea where that gate would lead. Did he?

"The Door, yes," Gail prompted. I set the question of Ben's near-escape aside (and why was I thinking of it as an escape attempt?) and focused on Conor again.

"So there's a legend associated with that Door, which Da knows better than I do," he began.

"You tell it your way," Niall said. "I'll fill in the blanks as I can."

Conor nodded. "Okay. The story goes that millennia ago, when humans first began to roam the Earth, the beings that had inhabited the place until then realized they were in danger. The creatures that had developed earlier – single-celled aquatic creatures, fish, dinosaurs, even lower species of mammals – none of them had the capacity to destroy the whole thing. They used resources, sure, and many of them could reason in a rudimentary way. Some were even intelligent enough to plan for something – in other words, they had the ability to set a goal and reach it by achieving several interim steps. But it was obvious that humans had the brainpower to reason their way into really big trouble – like overfishing a sea, or picking so many berries that there weren't enough seeds to replace the plants that died from year to year.

"They were greedy," said Rufus.

"Yes. And their solution wasn't to rein themselves in, but to simply move somewhere else. The Earth knew that strategy wouldn't work forever – her space was finite. And so she asked the Elementals to create a solution.

The idea they came up with was a Tool that would reset the Earth when the time came. And so that the Tool wasn't used too soon by some unscrupulous creature, they locked it away in a vault. The Door to the vault was made of a substance that was impervious to every Element, and it locked with four Keys, one for each Element. The Keys were entrusted to guardian Elementals. The theory was that the Elementals would have to agree that the situation was so dire that the Door had to be opened.

"But what if someone or something decided to steal all the Keys?" I asked. "I mean, that's what's happened here."

Niall took up the narrative. "We did think of that. That's why the guardianship rotates on an irregular schedule. And that's also why the Keys are periodically moved."

"So why is it necessary for us to be half-human?" That was Rufus.

"You're the link," Conor said. "When the time comes to push reset, humans have to be represented. Some human needs to agree that the Earth is so far gone that a reset is the only way."

We exchanged surprised glances. "It's not, though," I said. "Is it?"

84

"Think about it," Niall said. "Will humans ever learn not to be greedy? Will they ever be able to live in peace with the spirits of the land?"

I had no answer for him – which, to be honest, was answer enough.

"Where's the Door?" Ben asked. He'd moved back into the circle – either because I'd caught him trying to leave or because he was fascinated by the story.

"Somewhere in the Underworld," Niall said. "That's all I know." He glanced at me, and then at Ben. I knew Niall and Ben had a history – Niall had once done something that had nearly gotten Ben killed, or so Kate had said. I wondered now whether it had been an accident. Maybe Niall had never trusted Ben.

Niall's answer wasn't good enough for Gail. "Well, who does know? How do we find it?"

Niall seemed to be on the verge of giving another vague answer that would just infuriate Gail further. But he didn't have to.

"Hey!" someone shouted. "Hey! There you are!"

The voice was coming not from the fairy ring, but from the way we had come. The understory here was thin enough that I had glimpses of the newcomer, and anyway his colorful clothing stood out against the gray. My gut clenched when I figured out who it was.

Sure enough, a second later, Allen Owings burst into view.

"Oh, great," Collum groaned.

"Super-dee-duper," I agreed.

CHAPTER 11 – WHAT'S IN A RING?

"Hi, guys!" Allen said with a wave. He put has hands on his thighs and bent almost double, breathing hard. "Whew! I had the worst time catching up to you!"

"Did you come through the fiery gate?" I asked.

"Yeah," he said, straightening. "Whew! That was crazy."

"We lost track of you," Collum said. *I* certainly had – I'd been so busy worrying about cutting the electricity to my house that I'd lost track of just about everything else. Collum went on, "The last I knew, you were talking to some of the firefighters."

"The commander, yeah. And then I had to file my story. When I started looking for you again – hi, sorry, could you scoot over?" he said to Auntie Helen, who agreed with an angelic smile. "Thanks." He took a seat with an audible *oof*, then slapped his knees. "So like I was saying, when I got all that done, I saw your *house* was gone," he said to me, "so I ran down the hill to see what had happened. And from there, I saw you three disappear through that portal. So I ran down to get through it myself before it closed."

"And you made it?" I said in disbelief.

"Barely. I've been chasing you all ever since." He looked around the group. "So what did I miss? And why does everything look so washed out around here?"

"You didn't miss a thing," I said. The less he knew about what was going on, the better.

Apparently Collum didn't agree. "Allen," he said, "this is my brother Conor. Conor, this is Allen Owings, formerly of the *Harpers Ferry Sentinel*."

"Nice to meet you," Conor said. "I've read some of your stories. Sorry I never got around to subscribing."

"It doesn't matter. I work for the Associated Press now." He stopped talking abruptly and turned nearly as pale as our surroundings. "Conor Barth?" he asked faintly. Then he laughed. "That's hilarious! These jokers told me you were dead. Murdered, even."

"I was," Conor said.

Allen opened and closed his mouth a few times, but no words came out. Then he fumbled his phone out of his pants pocket and stared at it. "No signal," he said miserably, stowing it again. "This is another one of those Otherworld places, isn't it?"

"Got it in one," Collum said with a grin.

"But we can get back, right?" he said. "Because I need to call my editor again in, like, an hour."

"No guarantees, man," Rufus said. "And probably not within an hour. But look on the bright side. We're all in this together. And we're not dead."

"Yet," Collum and Conor chorused.

"So what's the plan?" Gail said, ignoring them. "Do we set up a watch at the fairy ring to see who's using it?"

"What's a fairy ring?" Allen asked. We ignored him.

"That will take too long," said Rufus.

"Or no time at all," said Collum. "We can't know. And we have no idea how time moves here in relation to other realities."

"This one must be pretty close to ours, given the timing of Allen's arrival and when he found us," I pointed out.

Conor shook his head. "Both time and distance are elastic here. Sometimes that walk from the beach takes a few seconds and sometimes it takes forever."

"And we know absolutely nothing about time and distance in the Door's reality," said Collum.

"Or unreality," Rufus muttered. "This is getting us nowhere. I think we should walk into the fairy ring and see where it takes us."

"And what if it takes us to Titania?" Gail said. "A fairy ring should, by definition, take us to the fae."

"Well, we can't just stand here!" Rufus said.

"Conor?" my mother broke in. "When you saw Damien, was he coming or going?"

"Coming," he said.

"And when he stepped out of the ring, which way did he go?"

Conor brightened. "I can take you," he said, and set off again.

I caught up with my mother. "Thanks for getting us back on track," I said.

She smiled. "I have some experience with Elemental arguments."

"No doubt," I said. "So…"

She tilted her head, inviting me to go on.

"Why would Damien have come to the land of the dead in the first place? Any ideas?"

"I can think of a few reasons. If Surgat is building an army, the dead would be a good choice."

"Because they can't die again."

"Right."

I shivered. "I don't like that idea. What else have you got?"

Mam laughed. "To be honest, I don't think he'd bother with raising the dead. He seems to have an inexhaustible supply of those clay men. No, I think he's using this realm as a cut-through."

"That makes sense," I said. "Surgat doesn't seem to be able to make gates the way Collum can. He can use static gates, though." I pondered that idea. "So the land of the dead isn't the end of the line?"

She laughed. "The way you mean it, of course it is. But the dead would come here through more than one gate."

I nodded. "Because if not, we would have seen a lot of confused newly-dead people wandering around that ring."

"And honestly, I think that fairy ring is an unauthorized incursion," she went on. "What use would the fae have for a gate into the land of the dead? The Fair Folk don't die any more than Elementals do. They create gates into the lands of the living to ensnare humans. They have no use for the dead."

"So we're looking for another unauthorized incursion," I said. "Surgat wouldn't want his comings and goings traced. He's going from our world to the fae to here to… the Door?"

"That's my guess," Mam said.

"That makes sense to me, too," Niall said from just behind us. He was taking his turn carrying Dora. It seemed to me that the child slept a lot. But then, if I hadn't seen my parents in centuries, I might do the same. Just the release of anxiety and the longing for comfort would be enough.

"I wondered whether the fae were on Damien's side," Gail said over her shoulder. "That annoying sprite seemed awfully anxious to get into Titania's good graces by getting in our way."

"What about Anemone?" I said. "And the other sylphs? Do you think Damien has them in his pocket too?"

"That's harder to say. Anemone was mostly mad because she didn't want us doing her job for her."

I glanced at Rufus. "And the salamanders? What about their loyalties?"

"They're allied with Earth," he said. "And those stubborn bastards are with us. Right, Leprechaun?"

Collum, at the head of the group with his brother, raised his fist in solidarity.

"So are the undines," Mam said, "and the other Water Elementals."

"I know the river spirits are on our side," I confirmed.

"And the Tuatha," said Gail. Two of the Tuatha de Danaan – the ancient Irish gods and goddesses – had helped us a lot in Ireland.

"And Damien?" Gail asked me pointedly.

I stared hard at her. "He's in thrall to Surgat. But I think he might be starting to regret that." I glanced at Mam.

"So you said in Hawaii," Gail went on. After we botched getting the Fire Key, I'd come upon Damien on the edge of the cliff next to Kalalea

Heiau, where Surgat had parked him while he delivered the Key to his master. "But I've been wondering why you didn't tell us about your conversation with him until we were back at the motel."

I blinked. Then I blinked again. "Are you suggesting I was *protecting* Damien?"

"If you'd told us when you met up with us," Gail said, "we could have gone back to find him. We could have finished this, right then and there."

"But Surgat was coming back," I said. "We were still recuperating from battling him. I didn't want to fight him again –not so soon after losing to him so badly." I saw her flinch and felt guilty – I knew she blamed herself for losing the Fire Key – but I wouldn't take it back, or soften what I'd said. She'd just attacked me, when we were supposed to be a team!

Instead, I plowed on. "It literally never occurred to me to suggest that we should go another round with him right then. And I thought everyone would feel the same way." I looked around at my teammates. Collum had his back to me and Rufus was staring at his feet on the gray dirt. I couldn't tell whether they were letting Gail blow off steam or whether they were suspicious of me, too.

"Besides," I said, "my head was full of some other stuff he'd told me. Family stuff." I glanced at Mam and looked away.

Then Collum looked back at Gail. "Killing Damien wouldn't have solved anything," he said. "Surgat already had three of the Keys. With Damien dead, he simply would have possessed another patsy in order to capture the Air Key. Maybe even one of us."

Gail grunted. "Maybe."

Collum looked at me and smiled. "I'm glad Raney waited to tell us."

I gave him a grateful smile in return.

Mam touched my hand. "I'd like to hear more of what he told you."

"I'd be happy to tell you – later," I said. *When we're alone.*

"Okay," she said, but I could tell it wasn't really okay.

As we'd grilled one another, we had moved out of the colorless forest and onto a colorless, featureless plain. Gray mountains stood as sentinels, seemingly miles away. I thought I saw a touch of blue along the top of the range. "Are we nearing the border of this land?" I asked.

Conor turned. "I can't answer that. I've never been this far."

Dora roused herself and pointed, her wet thumb glistening. "Look! It's a birdie!"

There was definitely something making lazy circles in the sky ahead of us. Moreover, it wasn't gray.

"That's no bird," Gail said. "It's a sylph." And she *whooshed* away. She materialized near the newcomer and led him back to us.

"Here you are!" he cried gaily. "We've been wondering where you'd gone!"

"Who's we?" I asked, our recent conversation about loyalties still fresh in my mind.

"Oh, no one," he said. "The clouds, the siroccos, the soft breezes after a summer shower…"

"You've come to rescue us?" Gail said, cutting to the chase.

"Yes! Precisely!" He lifted off and pirouetted in the air above us. It was like he couldn't contain his glee.

Rufus eyed this performance. "He's a sylph, all right," he said. "Brainless."

Gail couldn't argue. "Look – what's your name?"

"Westerly," he said, and landed. "You may call me Wes."

"Wes," she said. "Look. If you're here to rescue us, how about you get to it?"

"Where are you taking us?" That was Collum.

"Do you know where the Door is?" I asked.

Wes hooted in laughter and did a few more back flips. "You'll see," he said, as if it answered all our questions.

"Can you take me home?" Allen piped up. "Like, right now?"

Wes looked sad. "No," he said. "I'm afraid you can't get there from here." He turned back to Gail. "Let's get going, shall we?" He bent forward and pointed, then lifted off. Sparkles flew from the tip of his finger and spread out, rising as he did. He halted for a moment and glared at Gail. "Are you going to help me? There are an awful lot of them."

"Yes, all right," she muttered, and began making the same movements.

With Gail's assistance, the sparkling trail not only widened, but it also seemed more solid. In another moment, I realized why. "The Key is helping!" I called.

She glanced down at the bulge on her hip. A line of golden sparkles began there and joined hers and Wes's, weaving in and out between them. She shrugged and concentrated on drawing her pathway.

"Step up," Wes called to us. "It's perfectly safe."

Mam and I stepped gingerly onto the Airy path. There was some give, but not as much as a trampoline, say. Seeing that it held our weight, we went ahead. Rufus bounded up after us, then Annie and Auntie Helen.

The Barths paused at the foot of the path.

"What are you waiting for?" Wes said. "Come on!"

"But some of us…" Conor began.

Wes executed an impatient flip. "No, no, no! I was sent to fetch *all* of you, and *all* of you must come!"

Dora grinned and jumped onto the path – and suddenly I could tell that her dress was red.

"Dora!" Conor gasped. Then he stepped up himself, and now I could see the neon green of the technical hoodie he'd died in.

"Are you…? Kate asked, her tone equal parts wonder and dread.

Conor paused and seemed to run through some sort of mental checklist. "I don't think so," he told his mother. "But I'm glad to be getting away from this blasted gray, at least. Come on!"

Collum stepped up and slapped him on the shoulder. The two of them began moving toward us, and their parents followed.

"Last one through is a rotten egg!" Dora sang as she raced to the front of the group.

Through? I looked up. High above us, a speck of blue shone in the colorless sky. "The gate!" I yelled, pointing.

With Dora skipping ahead and Allen Owings trailing, we rose toward the glittering blue portal in the sky. I didn't know where it led, but it felt like progress anyway.

Chapter 12 – From One Otherworld to Another

It was a long, long way up to that portal.

To pass the time, we told jokes and sang songs. I taught Dora the theme songs to a couple of kids' TV shows – *Dora the Explorer*, of course, and *Barney*. I didn't bother explaining the significance of Barney to this enterprise – to help protect Conor's thumb drive, I'd created a decoy drive containing Barney's greatest hits – but I caught Collum's slow smile when I brought up the purple dinosaur, and that was good enough for me.

"How many parallel universes are there?" Rufus asked at one point. "Anybody know?"

"There are a number of schools of thought on that," Niall said.

"How many schools of thought, Da?" Conor asked. His color was looking better, the higher we went.

"A lot," Niall said evenly. "Billions, I think the last estimate was."

"Did… did you say billions with a B?" Allen asked.

"That's only an estimate, you understand," Niall said. "But it's based on sound mathematical calculation. Or so I'm told."

"So Wes," I called. "Which of the billions of Otherworlds are you taking us to?"

He stuck his tongue through his lips, as if drawing the path required all of his concentration.

I rolled my eyes and taught Dora another song.

I could tell we were getting closer – the portal had looked like a tiny blue pinprick from the ground, but it was beginning to look big enough to crawl through. Pretty soon, it appeared big enough for Dora to pass through without banging her head. I briefly wondered what would happen if your head ran into the top of such a construct – whether the border would bend enough to let you through or whether it would scrape off the top of your skull. How much would inattention cost you at the crossing? Would you bounce through, get a bad haircut, or lose your head entirely?

And then we were there. "Watch your step," Wes said brightly. "There's a step down just on the other side."

"How far down is that first step?" Rufus asked, eyes gleaming with mischief.

Wes ignored him as he encouraged the rest of us through the hole. "Careful now!"

I had meant to push the dividing wall with a fingertip, to see how much it would give. But when we got there, I was so busy watching my step that I forgot.

We stepped down onto a landing that was wide enough for everyone. A grand staircase unrolled before us. I was grateful to see that we weren't nearly as far from the ground or floor on this side as we had been in the land of the dead.

This new Otherworld was the complete opposite of the land of the dead. Here, everything was bright – the colors, the scents, the sounds. Dora – who turned out to be a redhead – clapped her hands for joy.

"Oh," Gail said faintly.

"You know where we are?" I asked.

She nodded toward beings flitting to and fro on butterfly wings. "The council chamber's that way."

"Council?"

"My erstwhile employers," she said.

My eyes widened. "I thought you worked for the U.S. government. I mean…"

"I did."

"You were a double agent?"

She screwed up her face. "No, it's more…" She glanced at Ben. "Oh, stop enjoying this so much," she snapped.

"She was on loan, you might say," he confided to me. "And she refused to bring me here."

Gail glared at him. "Because you would have done exactly what you're doing now – telling unauthorized persons things they have no need to know."

In a stage whisper, he told me, "She likes keeping secrets. It makes her feel important."

Gail drew back as if he'd slapped her. Without a word, she descended the staircase.

Ben winked at me and followed her.

I turned to find Auntie Helen at my elbow. "What an odd couple," she said.

"I don't know that they've ever been a couple," I said. "Just work partners, Gail said."

"Oh, no," she said, her eyes on them. "They mean more than that to each other."

As soon as she said it, I knew immediately that she was right. I mean, I'd noticed Gail posturing before this – the Lycra catsuit, for one thing, plus that whole three-point superhero landing at the fiery portal. Now she was walking ahead of Ben, back straight and head held high, as if she owned the place. And he was just happy to be with her.

"Huh," I said, resisting the urge to kick myself that I hadn't figured it out before now. Emotions are kind of my thing, after all. But then I'd had a lot of feelings of my own to distract me.

With a sly smile, Auntie Helen waggled her eyebrows at me. Then she descended the stairs on Rufus's arm. Annie beamed at him from behind.

"You need help, Mam?" I said, nodding toward our Madman and his Hawaiian auntie.

"*Pfft*," she said, and trotted down alone.

"Come, come," Wes sang out. "We can't keep the council waiting, can we?" He fluttered past us, racing Dora down, with Niall and Kate in hot pursuit.

Aaron went next. He concentrated so hard on looking around, wide-eyed, and muttering into his cell phone that I was sure he would miss a step and tumble to the bottom, taking out everyone in front of him on the way. Somehow, however, he managed to keep his feet.

That left Collum, Conor, and me. With a collective shrug, we headed down.

The council chamber wasn't far, thank goodness. I couldn't remember the last time I'd eaten, let alone slept, and I was past exhausted. As soon as we were inside, I sank down onto the nearest cushioned bench – although an observer might have termed it less of a "sink down" and more of a "drop and sprawl." The brothers Barth took up seats on either side of me.

"You okay?" Collum said, lacing his fingers through mine.

"Fine. Just tired." I rested my forehead on his and we exchanged a kiss.

"Me, too. And hungry. I wonder how long it's been…"

I put a finger against his lips. "Don't. That way lies madness."

He grinned. "I'm surprised Rufus isn't complaining."

"Maybe young love is sustaining him," I said.

Collum eyed me skeptically.

"Yeah, maybe not." We shared a laugh. I didn't think we were too loud, but Kate turned around and shushed us anyway.

The chamber had tiered seating, so I didn't have any trouble seeing what was going on. Five beings sat at a table on the dais below us. Four were Elementals: a sylph, a salamander, a gnome and an undine. I didn't recognize any of them, which didn't surprise me. Politics was never my thing. The fifth was Cassius Kimball, the personification of Aether.

"Elemental Team, we bid you welcome. Approach," said Cassius.

I stifled a groan as I got back on my feet. We went single file down the narrow aisle: Gail, Rufus, Collum, and me. "Hi, Cassius," I said when we reached the dais.

He inclined his head. "Please, sit. You've all come a long way."

"Thanks," said Rufus as he took a seat on the bench right in front of the council. "I don't suppose you have anything to eat, do you?"

Collum elbowed me. I shrugged as surreptitiously as I could. *I guess young love isn't that sustaining, after all.*

"We'll have refreshments shortly," said the salamander.

Maybe I should pause here to explain why I'm calling the council members *beings* instead of *people*. The salamander was one of the largest lizards I'd ever seen – on the order of a Komodo dragon, which I'd seen once in a zoo. A regular chair wouldn't have worked, so someone had rigged up a slanted platform where the council member could sort of lie on his belly with his front legs on table. And by the way, while I'm referring to him as male, I never found out for sure what his gender was.

The others were more straightforwardly humanoid. The gnome was a stereotypical gnome, or anyway he appeared to be more stereotypically gnomish than Niall – their builds were very similar, but while the Barths wore normal human clothing, the Earth Elemental wore a pointed green cap, a red tunic, and a hammer and chisel in his belt. His hair and beard were iron gray. He struck me as much older than Niall, who was many, many centuries old. Collum had once told me he himself had been born in 1532, even though he didn't look older than his mid-thirties.

The team still hadn't had enough down time for me to ponder that factoid and decide how I felt about it.

The sylph looked a lot like Anemone, except she was blond and wore a bright yellow dress. Also unlike Anemone, she wasn't angry with us – she actually looked quite kind. She, too, looked to be older than any other sylph I'd ever met. And she didn't sit in her chair so much as perch on the edge, lifting herself up and off with a fluttering of her wings now and then.

Mam had once told me that undines need more time in our Element as we age. The undine on the Elemental council must have been very old indeed, for she stayed half-submerged in an attractive water tank most of the time. In the water, her body was iridescent, and reflected all the colors of the sea – blue, green, and quicksilver. When she came up out of the tank, she was mostly purple.

Cassius looked exactly as he had the other couple of times I'd seen him: dark-skinned, built like a weightlifter, and with eyes that appeared depthless. "I'm sure you have questions," he said now.

"*I* certainly do," Gail said. "Whose idea was the detour through the land of the dead?"

"Mine," Cassius said.

"So you sent the golems?"

"No. Nor did I summon those dear to you to Malibu." He lifted his arm toward our human guests – excluding Aaron, I supposed.

"So who did?" Rufus asked. "Surgat?"

Cassius nodded once. "The demon wants you to approach the Door as soon as possible. He wants to trick you into giving up the Air Key – or else wrest it from you by main force."

"I'm not giving it up," said Gail.

Cassius smiled mysteriously. "Good."

"So this detour of yours," said Collum. "Why the land of the dead?"

"It was necessary," Cassius said.

"I got that part," Collum said. "Why?"

The gnome spoke up. "It is not necessary for you to know that to ensure the success of your mission!"

Gail rolled her eyes. "Secrets and more secrets. As usual." She leaned forward in her seat. "Come on, Lars. Give us a hint, at least."

The gnome eyed her stubbornly. He looked so much like Collum when *he* went stone-faced that I thought it must be a gnomish trait. "I see you are still impertinent, sylph."

Gail smiled. "Of course. It's one of my best features."

Lars snorted. "Hear this, then: The gnome will have need of his dead in this fight. All of you must have strong seconds in the fight to come." He stood and raised his fist. "Reasons to live. Reasons to fight on."

"Oh, don't be so dramatic, Lars," the council sylph said.

"They must know the importance of the occasion, Forsythia," Lars shot back.

"Yeah, we're aware that it's important," I said. "That whole 'saving the Earth' thing kind of gave it away."

The council undine smiled at me. "I like your spunk – Raney, is it?"

"Yes, ma'am," I said.

She inclined her head. "I watched your mother grow up. She has done well in raising you."

"Thank you, Cordelia," Mam called.

Cordelia waved to her and smiled. "After this is over, we need to catch up," she said.

"I'm looking forward to it," Mam said.

The sylph turned back to me. "You should know that I argued for your inclusion on this mission and won – despite your unfortunate human parentage."

"Don't tell tales, Forsythia," the salamander said. "She was included *because of* her human parentage." His head swung around to face us. "You all were."

The undine said, "You are right, of course, Volos," and slid back under water. From there, she regarded us with unblinking eyes. It was only a little unnerving. Okay, it was a lot unnerving.

"What are we supposed to do now?" I blurted. Everyone turned to look at me. "I mean, I know we're supposed to keep Damien from opening the Door. How do we do it? How do we find it, even? What does it look like?"

Cassius grinned mysteriously. "Do not worry, undine. You will not have to find the Door on your own."

"Why is that?"

"Because Damien will find us first," Rufus said. "He always has."

"Good point," said Collum. "And he knows we have the Air Key. So he'll be eager to engage us so he can take the final Key from us."

100

"Really?" Gail said. "This is Surgat we're talking about. That demon is going to try to *trick* us into giving up the Air Key. They'll lead us right to the Door."

All that made sense to me. "So what we really need is help with fighting them."

Lars spread his arms. "Ask and we will do our best to provide you with what you need. We are already in your debt."

"Salamanders to fight the golems," Rufus said instantly. "Surgat is animating them with live coals in their bellies. They're easy to disable if you can hit them fast."

"And you have to do it all at once," I added. "They have some method of communication. They're able to change tactics when a member of their squad is down."

"Surgat has also figured out a way to reshape them," Collum said. "We went up against some in our world with hard outer shells and flamethrowers for arms."

"It would be terrific if we could track down where he's making them and disable the facility," Gail said.

"Or destroy it," Rufus said.

The council members traded a look. "Done," said Forsythia. "We can spare a troop of Elementals to accompany you. And we can send a team to track down this manufacturing facility and put it out of commission."

"Anything else?" Cassius asked.

"I want to find Surgat's master," I said. "Damien told me his name is Signor Domenico Buffon. He told Damien he was a dealer in antiquities. That's how he came into possession of the bottle Surgat was trapped in."

The council members eyed me skeptically. "And you believed him?" asked Forsythia.

I raised my hands helplessly. "Kind of? I'm pretty sure Damien believed him – or anyway, he did at the time." I frowned. "You think Signor Buffon isn't the guy's real name?"

"Very likely not," said Forsythia. "It sounds like a play on the word *buffoon*. A jester or joker." She leaned forward, fluttering up out of her seat with her hand on her chin. "Does that sound like anyone you know?"

"Nope," I admitted.

"But then you didn't realize the fiery gate was in Malibu until your house was gone," Collum pointed out.

"True. I guess I can only think creatively when it comes to emotions," I said. "But I'll see what I come up with."

"Fair enough." She fluttered back down.

"Is that everything?" asked Cassius.

"Some food would be good," Rufus reminded him.

"And sleep," I said. "Some time to rest, at least."

Cassius laughed. "Your needs are very simple. So be it. Westerly will show you to your rooms. You may refresh yourselves while we assemble the other things you require."

Wes flew down from the top of the tiered seats, motioning to our companions. "Come, all of you! Follow me!" He waited, smiling gaily, while our families and friends made their way to us. Then he led us all through a door on the opposite side of the chamber. As we passed through it into the bowels of the building, I heard applause, and turned. All four council members, plus Cassius, were giving us a standing ovation.

Ever the entertainer, I smiled and bowed before making my exit, stage right.

CHAPTER 13 – PREPARATIONS

It rapidly became clear that the Elemental Council didn't have very many visitors of the human persuasion, whether fully human, only half, or simply kind of shaped like one. The food was fine – nothing too exotic, and served on normal plates in a room that reminded me of a cafeteria – but the sleeping rooms were a little quirky.

Collum and I surveyed our room with something like dismay. We'd gotten used to making do – pushing twin beds together to make a king-size bed, for example, and taking turns rolling into the crack while we slept – but this was the first time we'd run into anything this useless. The gnomish bed was far too short and narrow for Collum, and I didn't even get a bed. Instead, I got a water tank, very similar to the one Cordelia used in the council chambers.

"At least you'll be refreshed," Collum said. "I'm going to have to sleep sitting up, with my back against the wall and my feet dangling off the side." He sat on the tiny bed crosswise and wiggled his toes. It really did make a decent-sized chair for him.

"There's nothing refreshing about being disassembled all night," I said. "And anyway, I tend to reassemble after soaking for long enough. If I don't wake up then, I'll have skin like a prune by morning."

"Maybe we should ask our pal Westerly for a bigger bed," he said.

"You think they'd have one in stock?"

Someone knocked on the door. "I bet that's him now," I said, "here to apologize." But it wasn't Westerly; it was Rufus and Annie. I waved them inside.

"What did you guys get?" Rufus asked. Then he saw our sleeping accommodations. "Oh. Yeah, that might be worse than ours."

"What did you get?" Collum asked as the two of them sat cross-legged on the floor.

"A hollow log and a grow light," he said.

I laughed. "Do they think you're cold-blooded?"

"I guess." He side-eyed Annie.

She took her cue. "Boy, are they ever wrong," she said with a sly grin.

From the doorway, Gail asked, "Sounds like a party in here. Can I come in?"

"Absolutely," I said. "So what did they give you to sleep on? A branch?"

"Pretty much," she said. "But I expected it. That's what happened the last time I was here."

I'd forgotten for a moment that she'd been employed by the council. "How'd they take it when you asked for an actual bed?"

"I didn't. I made do with the tree." Her lips quirked up. "At the time, I carried a length of waterproof cloth as part of my kit. I tied the ends to opposite branches and used it as a sort of hammock."

"Smart thinking," Annie said. "I bet you slept great."

Gail laughed shortly. "Except the knots slid down the branches overnight, and I ended up with my butt resting on the ground." She shook her head. "I can't even do that this time – I turned in that length of cloth with the rest of my gear when I retired."

"Well, we have to do something," I said. "Who wants to find Wes?"

"I'll go," Gail said. "Maybe I can talk sense into him." She headed back out.

I went to the door and called after her, "Remind them that we have a couple of normal humans, too." She did a one-eighty, saluted me, and resumed her mission.

"I have faith in Gail," Annie said as I crossed the room to Collum and sat on his lap. "She'll get it straightened out for us."

"Our Windy is a badass," Rufus agreed.

I smirked as a thought occurred to me.

"And what's that face for, Madam Torrent?" Collum said.

"I wonder what they gave Allen Owings," I said.

"A bed," Allen said the next morning at breakfast.

"A regular bed?" I said, trying to hide my disappointment.

"Yeah," he said. "First nearly normal thing that's happened since I crossed through that ring of fire."

Ben Gelber nodded as he speared a bite of pancake. "I got a regular bed, too." He put the pancake in his mouth, chewed, and swallowed.

The four of us exchanged surprised looks. "I guess we're just super special," Collum said.

"I guess so," Rufus said. "Raney, are you going to want the rest of…"

Before he could get any farther, I handed over my plate.

"Don't *do* that," Annie said to me, dead serious. "Don't let him get away with that anymore."

"She wasn't going to eat it," Rufus said defensively. "And I didn't just take it – I asked first."

"I'm making it my mission in life to break you from cleaning every plate," Annie said.

"Uh-oh," Collum said with a grin. "Sounds like trouble, Rufus. Maybe you should get out now, while the getting's good."

Annie trained a glare on Rufus. "Don't you dare."

After breakfast, we met with our recruits for the Elemental Golem Strike Force. The council had assigned us about forty beings, mostly salamanders but with a smattering of other Elemental types.

First, Rufus and I explained golem anatomy. Wes had found a bunch of clay somewhere, so we fashioned it into a mini-golem and showed our troops exactly where to strike and what they needed to remove to disable the creatures.

Then Collum explained the golems' apparent ability to morph as the situation dictated. He told them about the ones we'd faced in Malibu – fire and water hadn't stopped them, and dumping them in a trench didn't work, either. Moreover, we hadn't been able to get close enough to one of them to figure out what made it so different from the others we'd battled. "Is the vessel some kind of metal, or simply fire-hardened clay?" Collum said. "The answer is that we don't know. We do know that regular bullets don't penetrate, but that's about it."

Gail continued, "So we're counting on all of you and your excellent observational skills. Elementals have been around since the dawn of time, yet we're hardly ever recognized for who and what we are. Some of us are simply good at hiding, but many of us have figured out how to hide in plain sight. Use those skills that have kept you alive for hundreds or thousands of years, and let us know what you learn about the golems. If you figure out where they're coming from, report it. If you learn how they communicate, or how they're taking orders, report it. If you get a bead on the location where the golems are being made, report it – we will have a team on standby to go in after them as soon as we get the information."

"And if you find out who is controlling the golems or where that person is located, make sure you get word of that to one of us as soon as you can. I cannot stress this one enough. We *have* to know the identity of the golem master."

Collum picked up the narrative. "Whoever the golem master is, don't try to take them out by yourself. Damien Jones and his demon are extremely dangerous. Their magic is immensely strong, but more than that, the demon will seek to mislead you and throw you off the trail. *Do not* go after them by yourself. Simply report in and let us handle it."

The council had provided some practice dummies for the recruits to use for punch-and-grab drills. Gail and Rufus stayed to oversee that, while Collum and I went to chat with the much smaller force tasked with finding the manufacturing facility.

This group was pretty evenly split, and we suggested to them how we'd been functioning as a team. "Don't be afraid to push your boundaries," I said. "Just because you're an undine who has never been a cloud, it doesn't mean you can't do it at all. I didn't think I could do it, either."

The group of maybe fifteen creatures murmured amongst themselves. "Yes, but we don't have your advantages," one of the undines said aloud.

"You mean being half-human?" I said.

"No," she said. "You were joined with the others in the Aether."

"That's true," I allowed. "But the first time I became a cloud, it didn't feel like I was breaking new ground. It felt like opening a door that had always been there, inside me, but I'd never opened it because I'd never thought to look for it."

The undine subsided, but she didn't look convinced.

"Look," Collum said. "The point is, you're going to need to think creatively and in unorthodox ways. Let's say you do locate the manufacturing plant and you find a way inside. Then what?"

"Figure out how they're made," a salamander said promptly.

Collum nodded. "And then what?"

"Take them out."

"That's right," Collum said. "How?"

The team members glanced at one another and shifted in their seats.

Collum smiled. "To be honest, I didn't expect you to have an answer. Even *we* don't know what the place looks like – we never had a chance to follow one back to its home base. Making a plan now would be a mistake. You'll probably have to toss most of it once you get the lay of the land, so to speak.

"So don't worry. You guys are breaking new ground here. You were chosen for this patrol because you're all smart, and because you're good at thinking on your feet."

"And our fins," the undine said with a small smile.

"And your fins," I confirmed with a grin. "The council is already proud of you, and so are we. So go on out there and knock 'em dead."

They'd already started laughing when Collum added, "Literally."

Teaching is exhausting, I discovered that day. I seriously thought about skipping dinner. All I wanted to do was collapse somewhere and either dissolve or sleep. Or both.

But I ended up being glad I went to dinner, after all. We'd had no time with our families and friends, and I was grateful for a few quiet hours to catch up with them before we tackled the next thing.

That's how I was saying it in my head: *the next thing*. Framing it as the big boss battle, or the confrontation we'd been working up to, was too much to wrap my head around. And *if we fail, Earth will be destroyed* was an absolute non-starter.

So we enjoyed each others' company and chatted about inconsequential things.

At last, someone yawned and set off everybody else. One by one, we called it a night.

My favorite gnome and I walked back to our room, hand in hand. Our path took us through a garden where sweet-smelling night flowers bloomed. We passed a bed of amazing white lilies that I had to stop and sniff – their fragrance was so heavenly. My romantic gnome picked one and placed it behind my ear. We kissed in the shade of a bower covered in Japanese wisteria.

As we approached the door to enter the council building, someone stepped from the shadows and blocked our path.

"Can we help you?" Collum asked.

Quick as lightning, the newcomer landed a punch on Collum's chin. He went down like a sack of potatoes.

"Collum!" I screamed.

Without a word, our assailant grabbed me roughly around my waist and shoved me forward.

As soon as I felt the nothingness, I screamed for help. But it was too late. The council building was gone, Collum was gone, and I was alone with this stranger in a dark place that smelled musty, as if it hadn't been used for a long time.

"Who are you?" I yelled, struggling to break his grip on me. "Take me back this minute!"

Instead, he opened an iron gate, pushed me through it, and clanged the gate shut.

Not a gate. A door. Attached to bars. I'd been thrown into a jail cell.

Moreover, I'd dug my fingers into my assailant's arm before he let go of me, and something of him had stuck under my nails. I brought my shaking hand to my nose and sniffed. It smelled like clay.

I knew then there was no point in yelling or struggling any further. The golem had its orders and had carried them out. Now it was moving away. It moved away for a long time before I heard another door open and shut. The noise sounded final. Too final.

The presence of the golem meant one thing: My father had captured me at last.

I wrapped my arms around myself to stay my shivering. A little bit of light – moonlight, maybe, or starlight – came in through a narrow window high in one wall, and I could just make out the parameters of my cell. No bed and no other furnishings. A bucket for peeing in. That was it.

Escape was possible – I could turn myself into water and ooze out through the bars – but where would I go?

Too overwhelmed and exhausted to think clearly, I propped myself up in a corner and went to sleep. My last conscious thought was a vow: if a rat came in, I'd turn into a puddle and drown it.

CHAPTER 14 – TIME HAS NO MEANING

I passed a mostly sleepless night. I mean, things could have been worse – the cell was cool but not cold, and the air felt a little clammy but not super damp. Still, my captors had left me neither pillow nor blanket, and I didn't possess the kind of magic that could have made the concrete floor more comfortable.

I gave up on sleep when the sky – what little I could see of it through the high window – began to lighten. As the day dawned, I was able to make out more than just vague shapes, and I was relieved to discover that I wasn't being held in some kind of crypt. In fact, it appeared to be a holding cell of the sort you might see in a sheriff's office in some Hollywood Western. The back wall looked sturdy, but the rest of the walls weren't walls at all – just sets of vertical iron bars dividing the space into three cells. The front wall looked a little sturdier, and the gate had certainly clanged shut convincingly the night before. But I wondered.

I got up off the floor with a groan and twisted to get the kinks out of my shoulders and neck. I used the bucket for its intended purpose. Then I took a tour of the walls of my cell.

A little poking, grabbing, and shaking, and my suspicions were confirmed. The iron bars were painted dowels, and the gate – while formidable in appearance – had a device attached that made the clanging noise when the gate was opened or closed. The locking mechanism wasn't even locked.

No lock.

I hadn't been locked up at all. It was all smoke and mirrors, designed to scare me. Designed to spin up the emotions of an emotional undine and leave her incapable of rational thought.

Boy, had they picked the wrong undine.

I pushed a button on the handle and gave the gate a shove. The clanging mechanism clanged and I froze, waiting for the return of my golem jailer. But after a minute or two ticked by, it was apparent that no one had heard – or if they'd heard, they didn't care. And now the gate stood open.

"She Who Opens All Locks," I said aloud, and grinned. I was glad that I hadn't wasted the effort to ooze out of my prison the night before. I would have been really ticked to discover that I'd gone to so much trouble for nothing.

I walked just a few steps before I spotted something white on the floor. I bent to look at it, and recognized it immediately, my eyes filling with tears. It was the lily that Collum had tucked into my hair the previous night – right before some mysterious jerk stepped out of the shadows, decked him, and dragged me here. To house me in a jail that wasn't a jail, behind a gate that wasn't locked.

The flower was crushed, of course – stepped on and mangled by an uncaring foot. I hoped Collum was in better shape this morning.

My tears dried as rage built within me. How dare he – whoever he was – do this to me! To *us*! To the Earth we were supposed to be saving!

I was no longer convinced that my father had been behind my disappearance. Moreover, I was beginning to have an inkling of who this Signor Buffon was.

Defiantly, I tucked the flower behind my ear again. Then I went off to find my tormentor and give him a piece of my mind.

I'd noted the night before that the exterior door had sounded as if it were quite a distance from the cell. Stepping away from the sheriff's office set, I saw I was in the far corner of a soundstage – a cavernous warehouse-like space with massive doors along one wall for moving sets and equipment in and out. I was pretty sure the "window" in my "cell" was actually a lighting fixture on a timer – but still, I was glad for it; that lamp and the emergency exit signs above the doors were the only lights in the place.

One of the exit signs was lower than the others. I walked toward it, being careful not to trip over cables and other assorted equipment, and discovered a people-sized door in the same wall as the big doors. It, too, was unlocked.

I pushed it open and stepped out, and knew exactly where I was: in an alley between two soundstages on the abandoned back lot of a movie studio in Los Angeles.

I had to hand it to these guys – they'd thought of a terrific place to stash me. No one ever came back here. Security only checked it out once in a while. There was no reason to patrol any more frequently – all the valuable stuff had been moved out. I'd done a movie here right before the studio shut it down. I remembered seeing moving trucks full of costumes and props, all destined for storage somewhere else.

I realized that if I walked out to the street, I could catch a bus for home. It would be a long trip, but I could get there from here. Of course, I didn't have a bus pass, or any money, or even my phone. Most of that was at my house – which, come to think of it, I couldn't get to by bus, after all, because it was probably still hanging out in some other Otherworld. And the phone was in my room in the council building, in a different reality entirely – although it would be useless, as it was out of juice.

Little bits and pieces of me were strewn all across the parallel universes.

My stomach growled, bringing my awareness back to my current situation. I was going to have to find something to eat, at least. And then figure out a way to get back to the team.

I began walking down the alley toward the street that would take me to the gate. *Is there anyone still here who would be able to help me? If I could find a way to get myself to the ocean, I could attract an undine or a mermaid and get some help from them…*

Something orange and white streaked past my shins, nearly tripping me. I stumbled but recovered.

As I got my footing again, I glanced to my right. And sighed. Loudly. "I should have known it was you," I said.

Tiger posed like a deity at the edge of the pavement, regarding me with huge, unblinking eyes. *Was that better?*

"Was what better?"

I didn't knock you down that time.

I had to smile. "No, you didn't." I dropped to sit cross-legged facing her and gave her a good skritching. "That was much better. And thank you for coming after me."

She purred and rubbed her head against my hand.

My stomach rumbled again. "Um, you didn't happen to bring me anything to eat, did you?"

Oh. Yes. There's a bag. She turned around and stretched, showing me her butthole.

I laughed. "Where did you put it, exactly?"

She righted herself and shot me a glare over her shoulder. *On. My. Back.* Sure enough, a bag was secured between her shoulder blades.

"Man, Gail is really good at this," I said, unfastening the bag. Inside was the Elemental equivalent of trail mix – nuts, dried fruits, and bits of seaweed – and my phone. I slid the phone into a pocket with one hand and popped a handful of trail mix in my mouth with the other. "Is Collum okay?" I asked while chewing.

He was knocked out, but he's fine now. He's got a bruise on his chin from where the guy hit him, but his beard covers it.

I breathed more freely. "And how's everyone else?"

Mad. Collum's madder than I've ever seen him. Ondine is beside herself. She keeps saying he should have taken her instead. Tiger cocked her head. *Does she mean Damien?*

"Yeah, but she doesn't know what she's talking about."

Tiger stared at me while I finished eating the trail mix. *Didn't Damien grab you?*

113

"I don't think so. Here, turn around – I'll tuck this under the harness again so you can take it back."

She huffed a big kitty sigh. *Demoted to trash collector.* But she let me hook the bag into the contraption.

"Hey, we are good citizens of Los Angeles County," I said, patting her head. "We don't litter."

So if it wasn't Damien, who... She glanced down the street – and as it happened, she was looking in the direction I'd just come from. *Oh. Him.*

"What?" I turned to see what she was looking at, and realized we were surrounded. As we'd chatted, golems had closed in from all directions. And at the forefront was a man with thick, black hair and an oily moustache.

"Good morning," he said, laying the Italian accent on thick. "Miss Meadows, I presume?"

All of our avenues of escape were cut off – except one. "Tiger! Go!" I whispered, and turned to rush through her gate after her. Except there was no Tiger. And there was no gate, which I realized when I jumped forward and nearly landed on my face in the dust. *What a time to remember to close your gate, cat.*

Signor Buffon was all concern. "Miss Meadows! Are you all right?"

I stood and brushed cinders off my knees. "You can drop the act, Stone. You're not fooling anybody here."

He raised his arms, palms up. "Act? What act? I do not know what you mean."

I walked up to him, took a handful of his impossibly thick pompadour, and yanked.

"Ow!" he cried, batting my arm away. "You have assaulted me! I shall call the *polizia!*"

"Right. You do that. And I'll then tell them how you kidnapped me last night."

"But *I* did not do it," he said slyly.

Technically he was right, but I let it go. Instead I opened my hand, showing an oily mess of black goo. "But you *did* do this," I said. I'd honestly thought he was wearing a wig or a hairpiece – it wouldn't have been the first time he'd disguised himself for a role – but the shoe polish and gel were proof enough for me. "Dressing up as an Italian antiquities expert to lure my father into a crazy, diabolical plot?" I flexed my fingers. "Um, do you have a tissue or something?"

"I do not know what you are talking about," he said, looking daggers at me, as he pulled an actual handkerchief from the breast pocket of his suit jacket and handed it over. He was even wearing colored contacts to make his irises look black – I could see the edges of the lenses and his own baby-blue eyes underneath.

"Actually," I said as I wiped the gunk off my hand, "I'm impressed by all this. You've gone to a lot of trouble just to get back at the girl who threw you out. Did you think this whole thing up yourself?" I plastered a look of admiration – no, starry-eyed adoration – on my face, and waited for him to react.

He preened, just as I knew he would. "Well, I…" he began, unconsciously dropping the accent.

God, he is so predictable! "It's just that" – I gave him an adoring smile as I tucked the soiled handkerchief back in his pocket and gave it a little pat – "I didn't know you were smart enough."

His face closed like a fist. "Miss Meadows," he said, the accent back in place as if he'd never dropped it, "you must be suffering from some kind of illness, yes? This is why you insist that I am someone you know. And I am coming to understand that you do not like this person very much."

"You got *that* right," I said. "I told you we were through. And here you are, back again. What is it with you? Why can't you take no for an answer?"

Now that he'd decided on playing the scene like I was nuts, he was sticking to it. "Poor, poor Miss Meadows. You must have suffered terribly in your transition here. Perhaps you struck your head? Hmm?" He snapped his fingers and one of the golems stepped forward. "Or perhaps you fell and suffered a brain injury."

"Or perhaps you should lay off threatening me," I retorted. "My friends know where I am. I expect they'll be here any minute."

"Excellent," he said. "*Perfetto.* Everything is going according to my plan."

A thought occurred to me. "You can't make a gate, can you?"

"What?"

"Where's the Door?"

Again, the sly look. "That is for me to know and you to…"

"It's not here, is it?"

He stopped dead in mid-cliché. "How do you…"

I began pacing in front of him. "Oh, it's easy when you know how this stuff works. See, actual Elementals can get from one reality to another by using gates, without having to pass Go and collect two hundred dollars or whatever. But you're not an Elemental, so you can't. Now, Surgat can transition between two realities, but *he* can't make a gate, either." I tapped my chin as I walked, muttering, "And his transitions must have to involve his master in some way. You can send him somewhere, or he can travel back to you. But he's not free to make his own way – you control his destination. And he can't go from one reality directly to another. He has to come back to you first." I dropped my hand. "That all makes sense. And of course *Damien* can't make a gate because he's all human." I stopped right in front of him. "And so are you."

"So?" he said, a little wide-eyed.

"So you need an Elemental to open the gate for you."

"The gate?"

I shook my head impatiently. "The gate to the reality where the Door is. Honestly, Stone, try to keep up." I looked behind him. "Where have you got the other Keys stashed?"

He backed off a step. "What are you talking about now?"

"C'mon, I know you have them. Damien told me Surgat gave them to you." I began circling him, trying to see if he was holding something behind his back, which forced him to pivot to keep me from getting behind him. "And I know you haven't taken them to the Door yet, because you can't get there without *us*." I stopped. "Did you give them to a golem? Or did you split them up?" I looked past him, as if I could tell by sight which of the clay creatures carried a Key. "Come on, gentlemen, cough 'em up."

"You are quite mad," he said.

"Not yet, I'm not. But I'm gonna be pretty freaking mad in a minute." I looked around again. "Where are my father and his succubus? They have to come, too, right?"

"Have a care, undine," came the guttural tones of Stone's pet demon. I turned in the direction of his voice. There was my father, with Surgat's ugly red head erupting from his collar. Behind him, I spotted another redhead: Rufus. He grinned and waved.

My heart surged, but I was careful not to let it show. Instead, I said to the demon, "Am I not supposed to comment on your sexual proclivities?"

"You know nothing of my sexual proclivities," Surgat growled.

"Don't I? Didn't you once offer to show me a good time in bed?" I strolled over to him and put a hand suggestively on his chest. "By morphing into the shape of my father?" I turned in sideways and leaned in close. I thought the turn might help me keep from gagging at the demon's signature aroma of sulfur and brimstone. "Or into that of a certain gnome?"

The barb was aimed at someone other than the demon, and it found its mark. "Enough!" Stone roared, all trace of his fake accent gone. "If I ever see him again, I'll punch him!"

Niiiiiiice jooooooob, Windy sighed in my ear as she breezed past me.

A look of surprise crossed the demon's face. "They are here, Master," he called.

"Take her!" Stone cried.

My father's arms pinned me, my back to his chest. "Perhaps we shall consummate this union before all is said and done," Surgat breathed in my ear. He licked my earlobe, sending searing pain along my nerves.

"Let me go!" I screamed.

"Now, Elementals!" Stone yelled. "We have your undine, and…"

"Her name's Torrent," Rufus called. "Get it right, you slimy bastard!"

"We have your Torrent," Stone resumed, as if taking stage directions, "and my demon shall do unspeakable things to her if you do not take us all to the Door this instant!"

"Order up!" Collum cried as he materialized inside the circle. He raised one arm high. All at once, our Elemental troops stepped out of thin air, surrounding the golems that were surrounding Stone, Collum, Damien/Surgat, and me.

Stone laughed heartily. "Order up? Really? You sound like a cook in a greasy spoon!"

Collum regarded him steadily until his laughter ran out. Then he said, "For your information, these troops are known as the Elemental Order. And we are about to make mincemeat of you." He paused to let the words sink in. "Let Raney go."

"Not a snowball's chance in hell!" Stone growled. "Do as I ask or your *girlfriend* will pay the price!"

"Why?" I said, bending nearly double. Between my burning ear and the demon's aroma, I was on the verge of throwing up. "Why are you doing this, Stone? Is it all because I threw you out?"

"You still don't get it, do you?" he said. "I'm doing you a favor!"

"A *what?*"

"Can't you see?" He gritted his teeth in frustration. "I can't believe I have to spell it out for you! Remember when I told you we could make a lot of money if you would just own up to being an undine?"

"How could I forget?" I said. "It's why I threw you out. You wouldn't take no for an answer. You wouldn't *let it drop.*"

"Right. You refused to take advantage of this golden opportunity that was *right in front of you.*" His smile was almost as frightening as his next words. "So I'm proving to you that I'm right."

"Wait," I said, horrified. "You're willing to *destroy the Earth* to prove a point about *money?*"

"It's not just about the money, Raney…"

"Oh, no. It's *all* about the money." Furious, I pulled at my father's arms. "Let *go* of me, would you?"

Stone nodded at the demon. My father's arms dropped to his sides.

I stumbled a few steps forward. Straightening my team t-shirt, I glared back at Surgat. Then I aimed my glare at Stone. "I was there, remember? I was *right there* when you made your pitch! Over and over and over! No matter how many times I said no. No matter how many times I explained to you that if I did what you wanted me to do, *my mother's life* would be in *danger* from *him*" – I turned around and shoved a finger in Damien's direction – "you ignored *everything* I said." I took a deep breath. "So now, because you have to be *right*, you're going to endanger all life on Earth."

"And it'll be worth it!" he said. "You'll be famous! It'll jump start your career!"

When he said that, I faltered. My career, after all, could have used a jump start.

But then, like the narcissistic jerk he was, he had to make it all about him. "We'll be rich!"

"There is no *we*," I said, as forcefully as I could. "No *you and me*, Stone. And there never will be again."

"No," he said, shaking his head as if he had a tic. "No. You still don't understand. There will never *not* be a *you and me*. Grab her," he said to my father.

A hand went around my upper arm. I glanced back to see that Surgat had pulled back and my father was back in control – or in as much control as the demon ever allowed him.

119

"Take us to the Door!" Stone yelled. "Now! Or I can't be responsible for what happens to Raney!"

"Not so fast," Collum said. "We left a few people behind." Staring straight at me, he cut a gate next to him, and through it came our family and friends: Annie and Auntie Helen; Niall and Kate Barth and their dead children, faded to specters in this reality; Ben Gelber; Allen Owings of the Associated Press; and Mam.

Damien breathed in sharply when he saw her. "Ondine," he breathed, as if he couldn't stop himself. "You are still so beautiful."

Mam's face gave nothing away – a good trick for an undine.

"I still don't know where we're going," Collum said to Stone. "Can't take us there if I don't know the location."

"We could follow the kitty," Dora said with a big smile. "She knows how to get there. She told me so!"

I found myself unsurprised. But Tiger had, as usual, vanished.

Ben tapped Collum on the shoulder. "I'll guide you."

Collum stepped back and stared at him. Ben smiled confidently. "I had time to do some research while you three and Gail were training your troops. The council's librarians were very helpful – they are in possession of a map of the known Otherworlds. I believe I can get us there."

"Gail?" said Collum, in a tone that made it clear that what he was really asking was, *Is this guy for real?*

She materialized a step away from Ben. "If he says he can do it, he can do it," she said.

"Well, okay, then. Lead on," Collum said to him.

"Just a minute," Auntie Helen called. "We're missing someone."

Right in the middle of the circle, Tiger popped into view. Following her came a green-and-orange gecko.

"Moe!" Rufus cried happily, crouching so the gecko could run up his arm. "Man, am I ever glad to see you!"

Moe waved to me and settled himself on top of Rufus's head. Of course I waved back – what else was I supposed to do?

"*Now* we have everyone," Auntie Helen said with a merry smile.

"At last," said Collum. He took Ben's hand and held it aloft. "Order up!"

As one, the Elementals in the outer circle made slashing motions with their upper appendages. With a tremendous *CRRAAAAACK!* we all crossed the veil at once.

CHAPTER 15 – THINGS JUST KEEP GETTING WEIRDER

We stepped out into what appeared to be a mountain meadow, although it was unlike any mountain meadow I'd ever seen. The sky was the color of lilacs, dotted here and there with yellow clouds. The vegetation, too, was off-color, the leaves too blue and the dirt below our feet too red.

Before us, a ring of boulders stood sentinel around a large mound of earth that was overgrown with blue weeds. Steps led to the top of the mound, where something unseen glowed.

In a blink, the mound was guarded by a cadre of hundreds of golems, standing in concentric rings. There were way more of them than our troops would ever be able to take out.

Stone waved his arms in a parting-the-sea motion, and the golem honor guard split to make an aisle. Up this aisle he walked; Damien, still holding my arm, shoved me ahead of him, so that I had to follow Stone. The golem guards reformed their ranks just behind us, cutting off the rest of my teammates and our allies, too. I glanced back and saw Collum and Rufus wearing identical looks of fury. Gail formed up beside them, glowering.

The golems that had come with us moved into positions around the perimeter of the meadow – just in case the cavalry showed up, I guess.

Then Damien shoved me again and I had to look away or lose my balance.

The earthen mound was maybe twenty-five feet in diameter and about the same number of feet high. Tangled vegetation covered the sides. The top appeared to be covered in blue-gray grass, and I still couldn't see what was glowing up there. There were sketchy steps on the side facing us, and

Stone made for those. I got the sense that not only was this site incredibly ancient, but it also wasn't maintained.

"What's causing the glow?" I asked Damien.

"What glow?"

"The glow from the top of the mound. Don't you see it?"

He grunted. "Shut your mouth and keep moving."

Which answered my question. Apparently only people with magic could see the glow. I wondered how Stone had ever found it in the first place, considering he was as mortal as they come. Then I remembered Surgat. It might have been the demon's suggestion to collect the legendary Keys and open the legendary Door.

"What made Surgat think of doing this?" I asked.

The demon himself answered in a gust of sulfurous air. "He wanted something big. Something iconic. I couldn't think of anything that would fit that description better."

We had begun to climb the overgrown sort-of-stairs. "And?" I said, to keep him talking.

"And I'd never opened it."

"Come on," I said with a chuckle. "Demons have bucket lists?"

The demon snickered. "Demons have no use for bucket lists. We are immortal. However, I do keep a lock list."

"I guess it's good to have goals," I said. "Keeps things from getting stale, especially for creatures who live forever."

"You have no idea," he muttered fervently.

Stone had reached the top and was waiting impatiently for us. I'm sure he couldn't hear what we were saying, but he definitely could see us having a conversation. "Silence!" he roared. "No more talking. Bring her here!"

So we made our way up to him. Stone had come to a stop on a ridge about fifteen feet from the base of the mound. The top was another eight or ten feet above us – it rose a couple of feet above Stone's head, and I knew he was five feet, ten inches tall.

Yeah, I know his bio says he's six-two. That's a lie. His agent wrote his bio. The sleazebag lied about Stone's age, too, and the number of children he's fathered. And Stone didn't have a problem with it.

And he wanted me to be just like him. Anything for money. Even destroying the Earth.

"You're not going to get away with this," Collum yelled.

Stone laughed like the B-list villain he was. "Who's going to stop me? You?" He laughed again. "I've got three of the four Keys *and* your precious undine."

"*My* precious undine." That was Damien. I yanked my captive arm and he let go of it. It seemed safe enough, I suppose – where was I going to go? Down the hill to my friends via a swan dive?

Stone stopped in mid-blather and gave my father an incredulous look. "What do you mean, *your* undine?"

"We had a deal," Damien said. "I deliver the Keys to you, and I get to keep my daughter."

"Wait, what?" I said. I stepped back so I could get a good look at both of them. "What was all that about Signor Buffon, and the demon taking possession of you against your will?"

Damien waved away my consternation. "Oh, all that happened, but it's not important."

"Not important?" I said, raising my voice. "Not *important?* It's important to *me*. Are you in this willingly or not?

"Let's move on," said Stone.

"We are *not* moving on," I said. "I want the whole truth and nothing but the truth, or no Air Key for you."

Stone's eyes narrowed. I could tell he was weighing whether to come clean – and how much of the truth he could get away with skipping over – against strip-searching me for the Air Key. Which approach would cause him less trouble? That's what he was trying to figure out.

And then my father crossed his arms and said, "Yes, Signor Buffon, let's hear the truth."

"Fine," Stone said icily. "Fine. All right. Here's how it went down." He cleared his throat. "I was making my way home after parting with Raney that last time..."

"After I sent you packing, is what you meant to say."

He cleared his throat again. "On my way home," he resumed, raising his voice a little, "I stopped in an occult shop on Central Avenue for advice. I hoped to discover a way to reason with this magical creature, since my words weren't getting through to her." I snorted. He ignored me again. "Stopping there was stroke of genius, if I do say so myself."

And of course you do. I rolled my eyes.

"I got the bottle and spell book from the proprietress of the shop. She even helped me develop my alias." He twisted an end of his moustache like a silent-movie villain, and the whole thing came off in his hand. I smothered a laugh while he stuffed it in a pocket. "It was Surgat's idea to collect the Keys. It was also his idea to get this gentleman involved. And it was the demon who... *introduced* us, shall we say."

"So it wasn't Craigslist, after all," I said to Damien.

"No," he said. "It wasn't. And I only got involved because I was looking for my heart's desire." He turned sappy eyes on my mother. She regarded him with no expression – again, a tough thing for an undine to do. I wondered whether the Elementals had sent a doppelganger in Mam's place.

"But then," Damien said, "I learned that I had a daughter. My only child, and a rare thing you are, too – half human and half undine."

"You wanted to collect me," I spat.

"I wanted my daughter," he returned. "I had no idea Signor Buffon wanted you, too."

"Well, I did, and I do. And I'm keeping her," Stone said. "This whole thing was my idea, so I get to decide how we split everything up."

"But she's not your daughter," Damien argued. "She's mine. And she told you she doesn't want you."

"I don't care! I'm keeping her!" Stone said. He was starting to sound not just stubborn, but nuts.

"Damien," Mam called. "Let him have Raney. Take me instead."

"Mam!" I cried. I wasn't sure what horrified me more – that my mother was willing to sacrifice herself, or that she was apparently okay with a crazy man taking me.

"Ondine," he breathed. "I've always loved you. I'm sorry for the pain I've caused you over the years."

"I know," Mam said. To the golems, she said, "Clear the way. Let me up there." And by some miracle, they made a gap for her.

"No, Mam," I said as she joined us on the platform. Damien pulled her to his side, and she actually seemed to like it.

"Raney," she said. "My darling daughter. This is the only way."

The only way? Was this an Elemental council edict, or something my teammates had cooked up while I spent the night in a fake jail cell? I looked to them for confirmation. Collum and Rufus seemed as mystified as I felt. Gail had disappeared.

"Is that enough origin story for you?" Stone sneered. "Yes? Good. Let's. Move. On." He grasped my wrist and began the trek up the final set of stairs to the top of the mound, dragging me behind him.

These stairs were in even worse shape than the previous ones. The treads were so covered with weeds and dirt that they were mere suggestions, and the out-of-kilter colors of everything were disorienting. I nearly lost my footing twice.

At last we reached the top, and I could see the thing we'd been searching for, all this time.

The Door was actually a hatch in the top of the mound. It was round, and it appeared to be made of wood, its varnish dark with age. It looked ancient, but pristine, as if time hadn't affected it at all. I supposed its inherent magic kept the weeds from overpowering it, the way they had the rest of the mound.

The glow I'd noticed came from the frame in which the Door was set. I couldn't tell what sort of material that frame was made from – it looked translucent, like plastic, although of course plastic hadn't been invented when this thing was created. Each quarter glowed in a different color: yellow for Air, red for Fire, blue for Water, and green for Earth.

The Door, too, was quartered, and the depressions carved into it for the Keys seemed to match up to what I'd seen in Auntie Helen's book. There were the three holes for the Fire Key's flames and the single slot for the hook at the top of the Water Key's giant wave. Over here were the conical hole for the Air Key's hurricane and the misshapen depression for the Earth Key's rock.

"At last," Stone breathed. "At last." He turned to me with a manic smile. "It's your cue, Raney."

"*My* cue?" I twisted my arm and broke his grip. "*My* cue? This is all your idea, Stone. You're the director. You wrote the script. You're supposed to tell *me* what to do."

"I'm surprised you haven't figured it out by now," he said. "You need to pledge your undying love for me, now and forever. Or the Earth *gets it*."

I heard Collum groan. "Not this again. Hey, moron – how are you planning to destroy the Earth when you only have three of the Keys?"

"Because Raney's going to give me the fourth one," he said.

I simpered. "You show me yours and I'll show you mine," I said.

"Raney!" Mam scolded. And okay, that sounded like my mother. I don't know what was keeping her from barfing at the sight of my father, but it wasn't that the Elementals had swapped her out for a different undine.

I stayed in character, though. I looked straight at her and said, "Really, Mam? You had no scruples about seducing Damien, but a double entendre has offended your delicate sensibilities?"

"I admit I've made mistakes," she said evenly. "But you're my daughter! I didn't raise you to talk that way!"

"Could you two settle this, like, later?" Stone said.

"When?" I said. "If you get your way, there won't *be* a later."

"Be that as it may, we're moving on," he said firmly.

"Fine," I said. "Let's see the Keys."

He glowered at me, and then at Damien. "Show her," he said.

"I don't have them, Master," came Surgat's sulfurous tones. "I gave them all to you, remember?"

"Don't tell me you forgot the Keys!" I laughed. "Oh my God, Stone, you never change. You've always been rotten at paying attention to detail."

Stone shut his eyes and stamped his feet. "Shut up, *shut up*, SHUT UP!" he screeched. "Stop making fun of me!"

"Oh, you poor baby," I crooned.

His eyes popped open. Then they narrowed to slits. His face turned purple and he balled up his fists. Then he took a step toward me.

"Ah, ah, ah," I reminded him, shaking an index finger at him. "You can't kill me, remember? You can't even hurt me too badly. You still *need* something from me."

He stopped, his shoulders heaving. "The final Key," he grated.

"Yep, that's it!" I said. "A gold star for you!"

"Give it to me."

"You haven't shown me the others yet."

I thought his eyes would pop out of his skull like a cartoon villain's. "What difference does it make?" he yelled.

"Maybe not to you, but it makes a huge difference to me. You've got me boxed in here. The Air Key is my only bargaining chip," I said. "Once I give it to you, my life is forfeit. Now, I could get you to promise that if I give you the Key, you'll let me go – but that hardly matters if you're going to destroy the Earth anyway. I'll die along with everything else on the planet. But if I get you to promise not to destroy the Earth, then you'll have me. Forever." I gulped. "Or at least until you die."

"Or until *you* die," he said. "You could die first, you know."

"Unlikely. Elementals are immortal, and when they mate with a human, their offspring can live an inordinately long time. Why, I know a half-gnome who's more than five hundred years old."

Stone regarded me with a raised eyebrow and pursed lips. Then he looked at Collum, who was grinning modestly.

"He doesn't look a day over thirty-five, does he?" I said.

Stone's gaze swung back to me. "You're lying."

"I'm not," I said. "Any number of creatures in this meadow are older than we are. Older and wiser." I leaned over. "More *experienced*, if you catch my drift."

He looked between us again, his rage building. "That's IT!" he yelled. "WE'RE DOING THIS, RIGHT NOW!" He fumbled in a pants pocket, cursing, until he brought forth a filthy bandanna. Rapidly, he unfolded the cloth to reveal a dazzling threesome: the Water, Earth, and Fire Keys.

I gasped. I couldn't help it. Each Key was mesmerizing by itself, but the effect of three of them together… The Water key shimmered with a blue and purple light. The Earth Key pulsed green and brown, as if in time with Earth's heartbeat. The Fire Key flashed orange, yellow, and searing white. And the way they wound around one another – well, it was clear they were meant to form a whole thing. Except there was a piece missing.

"All right?" Stone said, pulling me out of my reverie. I didn't come back willingly – my own heart had begun beating in time with the fluctuations of the Keys' light. He had to grab my chin and yank my gaze away from the Keys in the palm of his hand. "All right?" he repeated. "That's what you were after, right? You wanted to see the Keys. There they are."

"They're so beautiful," I said, my eyes drifting back of their own accord. "And there's so much power behind them."

He stared at me in surprise, and looked harder at the Keys in his hand. And I realized that just like with the glow from the trim ring around the Door, you had to have magic to see the Keys' colors and movement – and Stone had none. Zero. Not even a tiny bit. He was so mortal, he was stupid.

No, not just stupid – *thick*. He wouldn't have known a magical object if it bonked him on the head.

Or if he held it in his hand.

Which gave me an idea. I didn't know if we could pull it off. I'd have to keep talking, and I'd already stalled for quite a while. Stone might get suspicious if I continued to babble at this rate. More likely, Surgat would figure out what we were up to and stop us.

Still, Barney's theme song began playing in my head.

Stone was stumped by my comment. "I don't see any power behind them, or in them, or anywhere around them," he said. "They're just interesting carvings to me. But it looks like they might fit in the slots on this door."

"Yes, Master," Surgat said. "That's the idea. If we fit the Keys in the slots, then the Door will open and you may then access the Tool of Ultimate Destruction." His eyes – my father's eyes – glittered with avarice.

My eyes widened. "That's the actual name? The Tool of Ultimate Destruction?"

Surgat-as-Damien shrugged. "More or less. The translation is a little rough."

"Huh. And here I thought I'd made it up."

Surgat frowned. "The Air Key, undine. I must open these locks. My very essence demands it!"

"And so you shall," Stone said, re-taking command of the situation. "Raney, if you please?" He put out his hand.

I stared blankly at his open palm for as long as I dared. Then I laughed in surprise. "Oh, wait! You thought *I* had the Air Key?"

"You don't have it?"

"No," I said, hands raised in surrender. "I've never had it. It's a sylph thing."

"Then where is it?" Stone demanded.

"I just told you," I said, raising my voice. I still couldn't see Gail, which meant she was probably doing aerial reconnaissance. I hoped she would catch my drift. "The Air Key belongs to the sylphs. I don't even know what it looks like, really." I glanced down at the hole. "I guess it's cone shaped, like a seashell? And maybe three inches long?" I laughed weakly. "It's hard to tell from the depression in the Door. It kind of looks like a tornado, maybe."

"You've never seen it?" Stone said suspiciously.

"Well, no. I mean, I've never seen any of the other Keys, either, until now. Damien grabbed them all before we could get a look at them."

Damien and Stone traded a glance. "So am I to understand," Stone began slowly, "that you've never seen the Air Key?"

"Oh, no, I've *seen* it," I said. "I just don't have it right this second."

"And who, pray tell, does have it?"

I let a tinge of exasperation into my tone. "I already *told* you, Stone. It's a *sylph* thing."

He closed his eyes to keep himself from exploding. "And where is your sylph?"

"Sylphs are thinking, feeling creatures, Stone," I said irritably. "It sounds like you think I keep them as pets."

"So help me, Raney," he said. I could see I'd come very close to the line. "You know what I'm asking you. Where is your sylvan Elemental teammate?"

"Oh!" I smiled, as if in sudden understanding. "You mean Windy." I made a show of looking around the meadow. "There she is!"

Collum and Rufus stepped away from each other, revealing Gail, fiddling with something on her leggings. "Sorry," she said. "There's a hole in my pocket."

"You can't have lost the Key!" Stone wailed.

"Of course not. Don't be silly." She continued to fiddle with the fabric. "I just had to go back and find where I'd dropped it. Come on… Aha!" She came up, smiling brightly, and holding up a yellow, more-or-less conically-shaped rock. "Here it is! The Air Key!" She began walking triumphantly toward the mound. Then she tripped on something in the dirt. "Whoops!" she cried, and went down – and the bogus Air Key went down with her.

"Whoops!" I echoed, whacking the back of Stone's outstretched hand and sending the real Keys flying down the side of the mound.

"Nooooo!" he screamed. "Find me those Keys!"

CHAPTER 16 – AND THEN ALL HELL BROKE LOOSE

So it turns out that "Find me those Keys!" is a little vague, as commands go, for a golem army.

Lucky for us, our army of thinking, feeling Elementals knew how to take advantage of a chaotic situation. While the golems milled about, uncertain of what they were supposed to do, our troops began executing the punch-and-grab maneuver that Rufus and Gail had drilled them on. In seconds, somewhere between a third and half of the golems were busy reducing themselves to piles of inert clay.

"No, no, no!" Stone raged. "Why aren't you fighting back? I need those Keys! Pick up the Keys and bring them to me!"

The nearest golem guard at the base of the mound cocked his head at Stone. He looked like a puppy who was sure his master was talking to him, but couldn't figure out what he was supposed to do about it.

"And where are the replacements?" Stone went on. "There are supposed to be replacements!"

That sounded promising. Maybe our elite team has taken out the manufacturing facility. But my hopes took a beating when Stone said, "Surgat, I order you to find out what's delaying the replacements."

"I cannot take this body with me," Surgat said. It kind of sounded like they'd discussed the danger of leaving Damien unsupervised before, which made me wonder again if I'd been right that my father had been trying to break free.

"Leave him! I order you!" Stone barked.

"Yes, Master," Surgat said. A dense gray mist detached itself from Damien and sank into the ground. Immediately, Damien dropped like a rag doll. Mam caught him and eased him down.

"I've got to find those Keys," Stone said, and began to half-bound, half-slide down the face of the mound without bothering with the stairs. Shocked, I watched him go. It was like he'd forgotten Mam and I were there.

"Go on," Mam said to me. "Go help your friends. I'll stay with him."

"Will you be okay?"

"I'm fine, Raney," she snapped. "Go now, while you have the chance!"

So I went. Avoiding Stone, who was still muttering about his lost Keys, I scrambled down the steps and joined the fray.

Most of the golems around the perimeter had been vanquished, and our troops had moved in closer to help with the sentinels around the base of the mound. Surgat must have paused on his way out to give the sentinel golems more coherent instructions, because they were now fighting back. The good news, though, was that we outnumbered this bunch, and they were easy to flummox. They couldn't concentrate on more than one of us at a time. So one Elemental would distract the target while another – usually a salamander, but sometimes a gnome – would punch through the golem's clay back and rip out his fire.

I spotted Rufus and Collum, who naturally had found the one halfway intelligent golem who could focus on them both at once. I jumped in between the guys and began to dance – pirouettes, twerks, anything to get the creature to concentrate on me. I don't think the thing had the sort of equipment necessary to appreciate my sexy moves, but I proved distracting enough that Rufus was able to get in a timely blow to its back. Moments later, the creature was down and crumbling.

"Thanks for the assist," Rufus said.

"I'll need to see that dance routine again later," Collum said, with a look that indicated his equipment was working just fine, thanks.

"I'll see what I can do," I said. I moved closer to him as we scanned the meadow for more golems and said under my breath, "Order up? Really?"

He shot me a grin. "Best I could do on short notice. 'Avengers, assemble!' was already taken."

"Good point," I said.

Rufus joined us. "We may have gotten them all," he reported.

"And Surgat's still gone," I said.

Gail joined us, whirling in out of nowhere. "Maybe our elite team is giving the demon a hard time," she said with a grim smile.

"I hope so, but I wouldn't count on it lasting forever." Collum turned to our army. "That was excellent work! It all went just as we planned it. Stay alert, now – we expect them to bring in reinforcements."

As the troops nodded and began scanning the area for more enemies, I said, "Where's Stone? Has anyone seen him?"

"Still looking for the Keys," Gail said. "He's on the other side of the mound."

"Let's see if we can help him," I said with a smirk.

"Everybody okay?" Rufus called to our friends, who were surrounded by a detachment of Elementals. The troops had apparently appointed themselves their honor guard – which made me realize that we weren't doing a great job of ensuring their safety.

"We're fine," Niall called. "You lot do what you need to do. We can take care of ourselves."

That made me feel *so* much better. "Why did we have to bring them, anyway?" I asked.

"Auntie Helen insisted," Rufus said. "I tried to convince them to stay with the Elemental council, but she wouldn't hear of it. She said they all had a part to play in what's to come."

"Super-dee-duper," I said glumly. "Let's go see whether our evil mastermind has found any of the Keys yet."

As we began to circle the mound, Gail said, "He's not going to find the Air Key over there." She patted the bulge sticking out from her hip. "Your decoy idea was brilliant, Raney."

"Barney's Greatest Hits," I said, with a smile for Collum.

"If it works on one stupid villain, it should work on 'em all," he said.

Like I said before, it's easy for an Elemental to find a missing magical Key – just look for the glow. Humans, however, have a much tougher time.

So I was completely unsurprised to find Stone on the far side of the mound with his back to us, scrabbling in the weeds within a few yards of all three Keys. We exchanged amused glances and went to work.

The Water Key was closest to me, so I picked it up – and immediately kind of wished I hadn't. The Key sent a feeling like warm waves running up my arm, aimed straight at my heart. It was as if the Key knew who and what I was, and was programmed to bond with me. Then I remembered its original guardians were long gone, and the spirits of the Potomac and Shenandoah rivers had been watching over it ever since. That is, until Surgat released it from its watery vault.

I'm not who you think I am, I tried to tell the Key. *You may end up hating me before this is over. I may not be able to keep you from harm.*

Undine, the Key seemed to sigh happily in my head. *You have already kept us from harm.*

Us?

But the Key pulsed once, twice, and subsided to a soft blue glow. I shoved it in the front pocket of my jeans.

Now that the Key's speech had cleared out of my head, I could hear Stone muttering to himself. "They ought to be right here. She hit my hand up there, and if they flew straight and true, they would be *right here.*" He moved over a bit. "But if they bounced and rolled, they could be *here.*" He crawled to a new position. "Or *here.*" He sat back on his haunches and wailed, "It's not fair! I *had* them! I had *her!* I was *so close!*"

I glanced at my teammates. Rufus, wearing a thoughtful look, was stowing the Fire Key in his own pocket. Collum seemed mesmerized by the Earth Key, as if it was regaling him with stories of Ireland in the days of Brian Boru. With one eye on Stone, I waved at Collum to attract his attention. He blinked and focused on me. Then, with a decisive nod, he put it in his jeans pocket.

Had the Keys claimed my teammates, as the Water Key had insisted on claiming me? Were we the new guardians of the Keys? Was that what this had all been about?

It couldn't be. We still had to save the Earth from total destruction.

Gail materialized next to me so suddenly that I jumped. "Sorry," she whispered. "Your mother needs you." She pointed up to the top of the mound.

I sighed. "I'm getting real tired of these stairs. Keep an eye on the guys, would you? They seem a little preoccupied."

"I see that," she said, and motioned for Rufus and Collum to move toward her and away from Stone. When they began to head her way, I trudged up the stairs.

After nearly tripping and sliding downhill twice, I muttered, "First thing I'm gonna do after we save the Earth is tidy up around here." And kept going. What else could I do?

Mam was watching for me. As soon as I could see the top of the mound, she waved frantically at me. "Raney! Thank God you're here. Please hurry! I think he's delusional!"

I crossed to my parents and sank gratefully to the ground. I hadn't been kidding about those stairs – I was tired of climbing this mound over and over, and of walking and standing and fighting and having no freaking idea what was going on. I knew if I stumbled across a decent-sized puddle nearby, I'd be in it in a heartbeat.

As I approached Mam and Damien, a fleeting thought occurred to me: I never thought I'd see my parents together, ever. I definitely never thought I'd see Mam worried for my father. Yet here we were, Mam with Damien's head in her lap. To be fair, he didn't look good. His breathing was uneven and his color was off, although that could have been due to the quality of the light in this reality. But still, I was worried for her. Had Damien somehow sucked her into his web again?

"What a weird day," I said.

"What?" Mam asked.

"Nothing. Never mind. Just a random thought."

Damien's eyes fluttered open. "Raney," he said, and grabbed my wrist.

I flinched – Stone had bruised me there when he'd dragged me up the stairs.

"Raney, listen to me," he said. "Open the Door."

I pulled away from him as if he'd bitten me. "What?"

"You have to open the Door," he said again.

This was beginning to sound like the sort of thing a demon would say. "Look, Surgat," I began.

But Damien shook his head. "No, no. Surgat's not here. I... I hear him in my head when he's away. We have been joined for too long a time." He winced. "He's still fighting your forces – they are tougher than he expected them to be." While hope surged within me, he continued, "He has drained me, Raney. I am no longer who I was. I think the next time he possesses me, I will surely die."

Why did that bring a lump to my throat? "Don't talk crazy, Damien."

"I'm as sane as you are. As sane as your mother." He looked up at Mam and smiled. She brushed a lock of hair from his forehead, a gesture so intimately familiar, as many times as she had done the same thing to me, that jealousy surged within me. I bit it back, though.

I wished I had the time to get the answers I needed from her. I'd have to talk to her later.

Assuming there would be a later.

"Let's start over," I said. "How do you know we need to open the Door?"

"I have... sensed it. From Surgat's thoughts."

I shook my head. "But Damien, there's a Tool of Ultimate Destruction under there!"

He swallowed as if his mouth was dry. "By whose definition?" He coughed weakly. "Surgat thinks the intent of the Tool is shaped by who – or what – opens the Door."

That set me back on my heels. I tried to think of the first time I'd heard about this tool. Was it from Shenandoah?

Yeah, it was the river goddess who'd told me. At the same time as she'd told me about the Tool and the Door and the vault where the Water Key had been hidden for millennia.

"Shenandoah told me the Door must never be opened," I said. "Why would she lie?"

He shook his head.

"She said Earth herself wanted us to keep the Door shut," I argued. "We chased you around the freaking *world* to keep you from collecting all the Keys – so that Surgat wouldn't be able to open the Door! Now you're telling me we need to let that demon open it?"

"Not the demon," he croaked. "You."

The Water Key shifted in my pocket.

I was literally speechless. My gaze wavered wildly, searching for something that made sense – and my eyes met my mother's. Hers were deep blue and fathomless. I'd never seen them that way before. They reminded me of the eyes of Cassius Kimball, the avatar of Aether.

The sounds of renewed battle reached me. "He comes," whispered my father.

I reeled away to find my friends – and to stem the tidal wave of new knowledge and emotion that threatened to drown me.

CHAPTER 17 – THE KEYS TO THE MYSTERY

Those few minutes of conversation with my father had given me a killer headache. I have no idea how I made it back to the Door.

Why would Shenandoah have lied to me? Because otherwise, she seemed to be on our side. She and Potomac had answered our call for help at Lost Falls. And they had taken Alex Drake under their wing, or maybe under their waves – oh, you know what I mean – anyway, the point is they'd rehabilitated him. He'd been a greedy, grasping, power-hungry politician before that. Now he was a conservationist or something.

I'd solved the problem of Conor's corpse polluting her waters, and as payback, she'd lied to me? Come on. That didn't make sense.

But wait – the spirit of the River Nore, in Ireland, had phrased it differently. More carefully. She had said, *It is our understanding that you are meant to stop the door from opening.*

Our understanding.

And she'd also said she didn't know who had called Surgat to Hawaii. I could see now that it must have been Stone; he was working there on location and must have discovered somehow that the Fire Key was on the Big Island. Which wasn't one hundred percent correct, but it was close enough.

Anyway, that conversation with Nore was the first inkling I'd had that someone other than Damien was controlling the demon. And Nore had said Shenandoah hadn't lied to me – or withheld the information from me, either. *We are only learning of this now.*

And then I remembered that the rivers weren't the original guardians of the Water Key. Some sort of arcane lore concerning the Keys and the Door must have existed at one time, but whatever it was, it had been lost. Maybe with the death of the original guardian.

Niall Barth may have known all of the lore – or maybe not. He may not have been one of the original guardians, either. It had never occurred to me to ask Collum whether his family had always guarded the Earth Key.

The aumakua were definitely not the original guardians of the Fire Key. The menehune had told us so, and besides, the aumakua could not have assembled Auntie Helen's book. And it occurred to me now that there may have been four copies of that book originally, one for each Key guardian, and the others were now probably lost to time. In any case, the book had nothing in it about the Door besides the positions for the Keys. Maybe nobody wanted to commit the information to writing and risk its discovery.

I supposed Anemone could have been the original Air Key guardian, but at this point it didn't matter. Either way, the responsibility had driven her crazy.

Anyway, the point I was grasping a lot faster than I'm explaining it here is that the river spirits may have simply *assumed* the Door should not be opened. The original prohibition might have been along the lines of what my father had just told me – the key to the Keys, if you will, was the intent of the bearer.

A tool is just a tool, after all. It's an inert thing, possessing no intrinsic moral value. A tire iron, say, can be used to replace a flat tire or break a window. Or bash someone's head in. The tire iron has no ethical imperatives, no standards to either live up to or ignore. Those lay with the wielder.

And *destruction*, too, could be misconstrued. I knew in my blood and bones that Nature constantly renewed herself. She would destroy a thing that no longer worked in order to create something new and better in its place.

So the original message may have been that the Door should not be opened *unless the bearers of the Keys have kind hearts and pure intentions*. Or something like that. Regardless of how it was phrased, though, bad things would happen if you let something evil near the Door with the Keys. But if the Earth needs a reset...

But did it? And who was I to judge whether it did?

My thoughts were starting to scare me, skating so close to Raney-as-messiah. I wasn't pure. Far from it. I'd done my share of things I had later come to regret. I tried to be kind, but I didn't always succeed. My motives were not always one hundred percent on the Good side of the Good vs. Evil scale. I could be blackmailed, at least theoretically. I could be corrupted.

Maybe I was being corrupted now. Maybe Surgat was working through Damien to turn me to the Dark Side with this Chosen One nonsense.

I looked over my shoulder at Damien. He didn't look like a tool of the demon right now. But give it a minute – a dark mist was rising from the ground between us, and I was certain my father would be on his feet again very soon. Maybe for the last time.

Shaking, I turned back to the Door. My friends waited there, and each held their own Elemental Key. They regarded me with compassion and with something like awe.

I remembered how they'd been entranced by their Elemental Keys – but come to think of it, it hadn't looked like they were having the same experience I'd had with the Water Key. Instead of bonding with their Keys, Rufus and Collum had looked like they were getting messages from them. Marching orders? *Raney must be the one to open the Door?*

Somebody needed to put a stop to this. I wasn't anybody special. Nothing had changed – I still was an out-of-work actress with no job prospects.

And a blue rock in my pocket that was pulsing to the beat of my heart. But never mind that.

I was about to yell at them to stop looking at me that way when Stone crested the hill. He'd used the stairs this time, which put him between my friends and me. A wild light filled his gaze, and he nearly drooled at the sight of what my friends were holding. "Mine," he rasped. "Those are mine! Give them to me!"

'No," said a woman's voice, and someone short and regal materialized between Stone and me.

"Ah! Titania!" Stone cried. "So good of you to come! I will have the thing you desire in a moment." His voice dropped to a growl. "Just as soon as I get these creatures to stop their infernal meddling and *give me those Keys!*"

As he spoke, I looked the newcomer up and down – from the top of her head to the tips of her pointy velvet shoes, peeping out from under her elaborate Victorian-era gown. Even before Stone finished talking, I burst into laughter. "You have an occult shop in L.A.? Titania, Queen of the Fairies, is a common shopkeeper?"

She regarded me coldly. "There are worse hobbies."

"Oh, absolutely, if your aim isn't to flimflam every human who walks in the door." Then I put a couple of things together. "Wait. Is *this* the secret you wanted us to pay you for?"

"More or less," she admitted. "I was willing to tell you where the Door was, for a price."

"But not how to get here," Rufus said.

"Well, the joy is in the journey, isn't it?" she said brightly. She turned back to Stone. "Mr. Wolff, I believe we had a deal."

"But I don't have the Keys," he said, trying and failing to sound reasonable. "I can't very well open the Door if I don't have the Keys."

"Well, tell your demon to collect them!" she retorted. "Honestly, Mr. Wolff, you should not need the help of the Queen of the Fae to figure this out."

He flinched from the criticism. "Surgat!" he rasped.

"What happens if he doesn't live up to the terms of the deal?" Gail asked.

"Tell her," Titania said.

Stone gritted his teeth. "I must spend a year and a day in Faerie. Surgat!"

I gasped. "That's a death sentence for a human," I said to Stone. "You know that, right?"

"I didn't have a choice!" he ground out. "*Surgat!* You *will* answer me when I call you!"

It did seem odd that the demon hadn't responded. I looked toward my father. He was on his feet, all right, but leaning heavily on my mother with his hands clenching hers, and it was obvious that a great battle raged within him. At times, his face would turn the demon's purplish-red, and occasionally his nose or an ear would morph, but the body part never stayed demonic for more than a split second. "He… *fights*… me…" Surgat said.

I was shocked. Damien was only human – he had no more intrinsic magic than Stone did. How was he even upright?

And then I saw my mother's eyes again, and I understood. I was horrified, but I understood. She was pulling power from the Aether and channeling it to my father so he could hold the demon in his body. Trapping him there. To buy us time.

Not a lot of time. Nobody could do that sort of thing indefinitely – they'd both fry, Damien first. But maybe it would be enough.

I was about to make some sort of inane comment that probably would have made everything worse – but then a freaking dragon landed between my parents and me, blocking my view of them. "Moe!" Rufus called joyously.

Auntie Helen slid down from the dragon's back, patting his rump as she touched down. "Thank you, Moe," she said. "That was a very pleasant ride." Then she reached into her tote bag and pulled out the worn leather book I'd last seen on Annie's patio table on the Big Island. "Well! It looks like we have everyone here. Do you have all of the Keys?"

"Yes, Auntie," Rufus said. "Raney, show her your Key."

I began to comply, but Auntie Helen waved at me to stop. "Just a minute," she said sternly. "What are all of these hangers-on doing here? Not you, dear." She smiled at my mother. Then she turned her best auntie glare on the faerie queen. "But *you*. You have no business here. Begone!"

"I do indeed have business here!" Titania said indignantly. "I've come to collect a debt!"

"*Surgat!*" Stone yelled.

"And who are *you* to order me about?" Titania went on imperiously.

Auntie straightened to her full height, a couple of inches over Titania's. "I am Healani, the direct descendent of Kane and Haumea through Pele. My people *made* this Door when the Earth was new. We made a pact with the Elementals: to create and preserve the Keys that would open the Door *only* when the time is right."

"You say you own this Door," Titania sneered, "but I see no proof."

Auntie grew younger. Her wrinkles smoothed out and her gray hair lengthened as it turned as black as night. Then she grew taller, until she topped Rufus by a head. Her eyes snapped. "I am who I say I am," she said, in a clear voice. "You would challenge the word of a *god?*"

A large crow flew in from nowhere and landed on the ground next to Healani. It shapeshifted into another woman, this one wearing a garment covered in Celtic knotwork and a savage grin. "That one knows better than to gainsay *me*," she said.

"Hello, Badb," Gail said.

The Irish goddess nodded to her, then to Collum and Rufus, and finally to me.

Titania seemed slightly panicked. "I am not here to cause trouble, great lady! I am only…"

"Silence!" Badb roared. "We had an agreement, Titania! A peace agreement between the Tuatha and the fae! You signed it yourself. And yet here you are, interfering in the work of the gods!"

"Will you let me finish!" Titania stamped her tiny foot. "This has nothing to do with our agreement. I am here simply to…"

"To collect the Elemental Keys," I said. "To keep us from opening the Door."

"To conclude a deal with this gentlemen," Titania said hastily.

"And the deal was for him to use the demon you gave him to collect the Elemental Keys for you," I said.

"Surgat!" Stone wailed.

Now both goddesses were looking at Titania, and neither one of them looked pleased. "Where is this demon?" Badb asked.

"How should I know?" Titania said. "Ask this gentleman – he keeps calling him but gets no response."

"He's possessing my father," I said, pointing to my parents. "They have him trapped there."

Healani looked at my mother with new respect. Then she turned to Badb. "We should untrap him."

Badb snapped her fingers once. My father's eyes rolled back in his head and he fell. Once again, my mother caught him, but I could tell she was done in. My eyes filled with tears of gratitude. "Thank you," I whispered. "Thanks to both of you for doing what you did."

"Surgat?" Stone said, bewildered. Then he turned to Healani and Badb. "Give me back my demon!" he raged.

Badb ignored him. "Go," she said to Titania. "And take your tiresome human prize with you."

Titania glowered at the goddess. "We are not through, you and I," she said.

"Oh, yes, we are." Once again, Badb snapped her fingers, and both Stone and Titania vanished.

"Where did you send them?" Gail asked, shocked.

"Back to somewhere in faerie." Badb grinned slyly. "I wasn't too careful." She turned to Healani. "All right, then?"

"Yes, we're all set," said Healani, as she became Auntie Helen again. "Thank you for coming."

Badb nodded to each of us, then shapeshifted into a crow and flew away.

Now there were just seven of us gathered around the Door: Auntie Helen; my parents; and Rufus, Collum, Gail, and me. Oh, and Moe, who was still dragon-sized.

"Moe, would you see about getting Damien and Ondine back to the others?" Auntie Helen said. "I'm certain Kate and Niall will know how to help them."

"And if not, Ben will," Gail called.

I ran to Moe to help him load up my parents. Mam and I managed to get Damien on his back first. Then I hugged her, tears running down both our faces. "You were so brave," I whispered.

"No braver than you," she said, and stroked my hair the way she used to. "I love you so, my darling daughter."

"I love you, too, Mam." We hugged again. Then she climbed aboard the dragon for the short flight to where the rest of our friends and family waited. They all waved to us atop the mound, and we all waved back.

Then I stepped to my position in front of the Water quarter on the Door. "Let's do this," I said.

CHAPTER 18 – THE DOOR OPENS

All I can say is I hope I never have to go through that again.

Auntie Helen opened her book and began reading aloud in a language I didn't understand. Ancient Polynesian, maybe? Whatever it was, it had an awful lot of vowels and glottal stops.

But while my human half didn't understand the words, my undine half caught the meaning. It took over in a way I'd never felt happen before. Oh, there had always been days in my life when I hadn't *meant* to find myself dispersed in a body of water, but it had happened anyway. Like at Twin Lakes when that ancient glacial water called to me. It had happened a lot when I was a kid, but you grow up and you learn self-control. You stop peeing the bed at night, you quit throwing tantrums in toy stores, and you stop flinging yourself into every puddle or ditch you see. You learn discernment.

Mam taught me discernment. I glanced toward the group below us in the meadow and hoped she was all right.

But I could only spare a glance, for Auntie Helen kept going. I looked around the circle at my teammates – my friends. My ohana. They all wore the same look of rapt concentration on the Door and the task before us.

My heart began to pound in time with the rhythm of Auntie Helen's words. I thought I heard drums – but no, it was all of our hearts beating together. Keeping time.

It was time.

Auntie Helen cried out in English, "Earth, unlock the Door!"

Collum lumbered forward, each step shaking the ground beneath our feet. "I am Earth," he proclaimed, "and I unlock this Door!" He slammed the rock-shaped Earth Key home. When he drew back his hand, a green tendril of energy grew from the Key, keeping him connected to it.

"Air! Unlock the Door!" Auntie Helen cried.

Gail took flight, executing graceful leaps and pirouettes midair before hovering over her quarter. "I am Air!" she sang in a high soprano. "And I unlock this Door!" She dropped the conical Air Key from a couple of feet off the ground. The Key twirled as it fell and settled into place, and a tendril of sunny yellow energy rose from it to maintain its connection with her.

"Fire! Unlock the Door!"

Rufus erupted in flame like a Roman candle. I could hardly make out his form within the fire, but there was no mistaking his voice as he boomed out, "I am Fire, and I unlock this Door!" As he held the Fire Key over the Door, the Key too seemed to be aflame. He brought it down and clicked it into place, then stepped back. A trail of fiery orange energy immediately sprang from the Key and tethered itself to him.

"Water! Unlock the Door!"

The roaring of my Element filled my ears. I opened myself gladly to the ocean, my true home. I flowed to my quarter of the Door, opened my mouth, and the voice of my Element tumbled out. "I am Water!" I proclaimed. "And I unlock this Door!" I bent, more gracefully than I'd ever moved in my life. I didn't remember pulling the Water Key from my pocket, but I must have done it at some point, for there it was, shimmering in the palm of my hand. I placed the Key on the Door and hooked the top of the wave into the hole in the Door.

"The Door is open!" Auntie Helen proclaimed, even though it was still seated in the glowing ring.

But not for long. Another moment and the Door began to rotate, faster and faster, until it resembled a roulette wheel. My human side asserted itself briefly and hoped we weren't playing the wrong game of chance. But then I noticed the tendrils that connected us to our Keys twisted around each other as the Door spun, creating an unbreakable cord of multicolored energy.

At last then the Door slowed and a tiny, round compartment at its center, where the carved lines delineating the quarters met, popped open.

Auntie Helen began reading from her book again, proclaiming things in that vaguely Polynesian language. Then she looked at me and said, "Water, retrieve the seed."

Seed? I leaned over as far as I dared and looked into the compartment. Sure enough, inside it was a single seed – and suddenly I balked. "Are you sure this is supposed to be my job?" I said. "Wouldn't seeds be more in Earth's line?"

"Water!" Auntie Helen barked in Healani's voice. "It is written! You must retrieve the seed!"

"Yes, all right!" I said, irritated. "I'm picking up the seed, all right?" But I wasn't. I couldn't do it. Water pushed my hand to the middle of the Door, but my human side refused to let it descend.

"Do you need help?" Gail asked.

"No one can help her! She must do it herself!" Auntie Helen warned us. "It is written!"

"Yeah, I got that part," I muttered.

"Want it toasted?" Rufus asked, a wicked gleam in his eyes. "I mean, it's probably not even salted."

"I'm not going to eat it, you goofball," I said, chuckling. Then I cast an anxious look at Auntie Helen. "Am I?"

"Retrieve the seed!" she cried. It was clearly the only answer I was going to get out of her.

But I knew now what was stopping me. Swallowing a seed puts it in your belly. Bellies are where babies grow. And I didn't want a baby.

This was probably something I should have worked out in therapy years before, except how do you tell a therapist you're half undine without them having you committed? And the half-undine part was significant. It was because of it that Mam had dragged me from one new school to the next. Oh, we were definitely on the run from Damien for all those years – but he wasn't the only person who could blow our cover. And Mam didn't possess the kind of magic that would have protected us from whatever unpleasantness our very human neighbors might have cooked up if they'd found out what we were. Rape probably would have been just the start.

Plus let's not forget the whole selkie thing. The man in the story had basically kidnapped her, and the kids they had together held her there as much as her inability to find her real skin.

And then I got into acting, where pregnancy can be a liability, depending on the project you're working on and how amenable the showrunners are to letting your character have a baby. For *Story of a Homicide*, it was highly unlikely that my character would be allowed to have a kid. The story line just wouldn't have allowed for it.

The bottom line is that for a lot of reasons, I wasn't interested in having a baby. And this business with the seed and *only Raney can do this* was sounding a lot like I didn't want to be involved.

But then Collum – my amazing gnome – called to me. "Raney, look at me," he said, and I did. "It's all right," he said. "We'll work it out."

I didn't actually fully acquiesce. But while my human half was considering the possibility that with this man, this amazing man, it might be okay… Anyway, while I was vacillating, my Elemental half snatched up the seed.

And as I stared blankly at the tiny thing in my hand, the Door began to spin again, faster than before. The glow from the ring intensified so that I had to shade my eyes with the hand that wasn't holding the seed. When it stopped, the Door was gone. Just vanished. And I could see, far below – probably at the level of the ground – a familiar shimmering. Water.

I knew what I was supposed to do, but I didn't know why. The Earth wanted me in that giant tank of Water, and I was supposed to bring the seed with me.

Something whooshed past me, making me back up a step. "Wheeeeee!" a child cried as she zoomed through the portal and into the tank.

"Dora!" Niall and Kate cried from below. Collum and I exchanged a look of surprise and panic.

His sister's voice echoed up from the depths. "Come on in, Raney! The water's fine!"

"Raney!" Collum cried. "You have to go!"

"I can't rescue her, you know," I cried. "She's already dead!"

Regardless, I knew I had to go. I *wanted* to go. But fear had me stuck fast in place.

That's when I heard a disgusted kitty sigh. *I have to do everything around here.* And a familiar, furry weight slammed into the backs of my knees. They buckled and I fell forward, yelling, flipping in midair as Gail had done just moments before.

With the seed still clutched tightly in my fist, I hit the water and immediately fell apart.

Although I'd never dissolved quite like this before. In most instances, I would keep my wits about me when I was one with water. I had held conversations with river and lake spirits, and remembered later what we said. I had tracked a gecko-turned-dragon thousands of feet below the surface of the ocean.

But this – this was like a dream. Or an acid trip, maybe. My consciousness seemed to fade in and out. At one point, I think I was singing Barney's theme song along with Dora. At another, I could feel the seed in my hand growing bigger. But it wasn't expanding by simply absorbing the water in the tank – it was absorbing something from me, too. It was like all the energy in that unbreakable cord had let go of Rufus, Gail, and Collum when I fell, but it transferred the connection to the bits of Earth, Air, and Fire that I'd gleaned from my team when we were transformed in the Aether. And now the seed was feeding from it, and growing ever larger.

The seed was massive now – bigger than the water tank I had fallen into. I dreamed I saw the seed split open and a tendril snake out. It looked like Dora, or so I thought in my dream. Then more tendrils grew, and more, and more – one for each of us and our families and friends – and

then still more came. There was a tendril for every person in the world –
not just human people or magical people, but the animal people, too. And
the plant people. And the rock people. The seed would renew all of it. That
was why it had come. And it had needed Water to grow, which is why it
had chosen me.

In my dream, I came to the conclusion that I'd magically given birth
to the whole Earth. And that was the last I knew for quite a while.

CHAPTER 19 – THERE'S NO PLACE LIKE HOME

I woke up in my own bed in my own beach house in Malibu.

I knew where I was because I could hear the waves washing ashore on the beach below. Even without opening my eyes, I could tell it was going to be a beautiful day. That made me smile.

Then I heard noises in the kitchen. Then I smelled coffee brewing. And then I heard Collum scolding the cat.

Wait. Collum? The cat?

I got out of bed and threw on a robe, then used the bathroom. By the time I was done with that, I could hear *two* male voices coming from the kitchen.

I walked somewhat faster than usual to see what was going on. A red-haired man was seated at the table with his back to me. "Collum?" I said.

He turned – and as soon as I saw his profile, I knew who it was. "Conor!" I said in shock.

Conor it was. He rose to give me a hug, which I returned.

"Why aren't you dead?" I blurted as I took a seat. Then I thought about what I'd just said. "I'm sorry. I mean... it's just that..."

Collum appeared from the kitchen, his eyes dancing merrily. "Here," he said, plopping a mug of steaming joe in front of me. "You need this."

"Thanks. Hey, get back here." I caught his hand as he tried to retreat, then stood to give him a proper good-morning greeting.

"Mmmm," he said.

"Mmmm," I agreed. "And there's more where that came from."

He kissed me again. "If I take you up on that offer, though, the eggs are going to burn," he said as he pulled away.

"Well, we can't have that," I said, plopping down again. "I'm starving. Um, where are we? I mean, I know this is my house and all, but where is it?"

"Back in our world," Conor said, over the rim of his own cup.

"So the house came back on its own?"

"Yep. Once it knew the coast was clear," said Conor.

I sighed with relief. "Well, I'm glad that's over. But… You're alive?"

Collum came out with plates of food. "Eat first," he commanded. "Then we'll get you caught up."

I looked back and forth between the brothers gnome. "How much did I miss?"

"A lot," said Conor.

After breakfast, Collum settled me on the couch under a blanket while he and Conor cleared away the breakfast dishes and started the dishwasher. "I can help," I called.

"You just rest," Collum called.

Rest? Not relax? I puzzled over his phrasing, but decided against trying to shout questions over the noise of the dishwasher. Besides, it felt good to rest.

"Raney?"

My eyes popped open. Collum was standing – okay, no, actually he was hovering over me, with my coffee mug in his hand. Conor had his own mug and was settling into an adjacent chair.

I fumbled myself into a sitting position, more or less. "Hey, thanks. Guess I nodded off." I took the mug from him and sipped.

He sat on the couch next to me, concern lining his face. "Maybe you should go back to bed."

I was about to offer my knee-jerk *I'm fine* response, but something about the way both of the guys were looking at me made me stop. "How long was I out?" I said instead.

"Nine days?" Collum asked his brother.

"Ten," Conor said.

"That's right. Ten."

I nearly dropped my mug. "I've been sleeping for *ten days?*"

"Mam said to let you sleep as long as you wanted," Collum said.

"You'd been through a lot," Conor offered.

"Well, yeah. But ten *days?*"

They both shrugged helplessly.

"How was I, like, peeing and stuff?"

"Your mother was here," Collum said. Which didn't answer the question, but I relaxed anyway. I trusted her in matters of undine hygiene a lot more than I trusted a couple of gnomes.

Also, it meant she'd survived. "Is she okay? Is she here?"

"She's fine," Collum said. "She's gone to check on a neighbor. She'll be back soon."

"A neighbor? Like, one of *my* neighbors? But I don't think she knows anybody else with a beach house, except…" Out of the blue, I remembered Mam's story about playing in the waves with a merman to attract a human lover, and nearly dropped my mug again. "*Damien?*"

"It turns out his house is just up the coast," Conor said. "Isn't that crazy? All these years, you've been living just two miles from your father, and neither one of you ever knew it."

"Crazy is one word for it." I took another sip and put the mug down. "Okay. From the top. What happened after Tiger pushed me into the tank?"

Between the two of them, I got a narrative that went like this, more or less: Collum was ready to go in right after me – both on my account and Dora's. But Auntie Helen stopped him by yelling something about how the ritual had to play itself out. Under no circumstances whatsoever was anyone allowed to enter the water tank until the transformation was complete.

"So I said, 'What transformation?'" Collum said. "I had visions of you turning into… I don't know what. But I was worried that when you came out, you wouldn't be Raney anymore."

"He thought you'd turn into Aqua Woman or something," Conor said with a laugh. "He thought you'd sprout gills and swim away."

Collum nodded in chagrin. "I did. Maybe not Aqua Woman specifically, but something unrecognizable. Auntie Helen was so adamant that *you* had to go into the tank – not any of the rest of us – that I was sure you would be sacrificed."

"The same thought crossed my mind while I was standing on the brink," I admitted. "But that's not what I was there for." I reached for my mug and took a sip of lukewarm coffee.

"So what *were* you there for?" Collum asked. "We've discussed it, of course, and we all have our pet theories, but you were actually there."

"Maybe I should wait and set everyone straight at once," I said.

"No, c'mon," Collum pleaded. "You wouldn't do that to your best guy."

I smiled. "How could I?" I put down my mug again. "Okay. I was the catalyst – the bridge between the seed and the water. The seed needed the water to sprout, but not just any water – it had to be Elemental Water."

"Magic seed, magic Water," Conor said, nodding.

"But there was more," I went on. I touched Collum's knee. "Did you see the energy tendrils that linked us to our Keys?" At his nod, I said, "And did you see how the Door spun them together?"

"I did. But I didn't see what happened to it."

"It went into the tank with me. The seed used it to siphon off some of the essence I got from you, Rufus, and Gail in our transformation."

"Like an umbilical cord," Conor said, wide-eyed.

Collum leaned toward me and inspected my eyes. "What color?" I asked.

"Still hazel." He leaned back.

"So we're still joined. That makes sense. I'd guess there's no way to undo it."

Collum took my hand. "Probably not. And at this point I don't think I'd want it undone."

I grinned and squeezed his hand. "Anyway, that's pretty much it. The seed sucked up all the water and germinated, with millions of little tendrils snaking out of it. Hundreds of millions, maybe. And then I guess I passed out."

"What about Dora?" Collum asked.

I glanced between him and Conor. "Did she make it?"

"No," Conor said. Collum just shook his head.

"I'm sorry, you guys," I said, and squeezed Collum's hand again. I couldn't imagine what it must be like to spend time again with someone you'd lost, only to have that person snatched from you. The pain would be enormous – worse, maybe, than losing them the first time. Even if the first time was centuries ago.

"Was she necessary?" Collum asked.

I knew what he meant: Did the transformation process depend on her being there? I thought about that for a minute or two before I answered. "I think she helped," I said finally. "I didn't get the sense that a child was *required* for the ritual to succeed, but the seed definitely drew on her childlike wonder. I think she made it more fun."

The guys both laughed at that, and Conor wiped his eyes. "That explains a lot," he said to Collum.

"What do you mean?" I asked.

The guys both grinned at me. "You haven't looked outside yet, have you?"

"No. Why?"

"Come on." Collum pulled me to my feet and helped me wrap the blanket more snugly around me. Then we paraded to the front door. Conor opened it and waved me out into a wonderland.

My yard had been boring grass with a few flowers and bushes in strategic locations. The maintenance on all those non-native plants had cost me a small fortune.

All of it was gone. In its place were stands of trees, fantastically shaped, with flowers in all the colors of the rainbow. I laughed and clapped my hands. "Dora did this?" I asked, turning to the guys behind me.

"I wouldn't be a bit surprised," said Collum. He rested his hands on my shoulders and I leaned into him.

"It's like this everywhere," Conor said. "We've been seeing it on the news. Trees and flowers in all shapes and colors, all extremely hardy for their zones. It looks like *Alice in Wonderland* everywhere."

"The Tim Burton film?" I asked. "Wow. That's crazy."

"The botanists are having a field day," Conor said.

"I'll bet."

"You haven't seen the ocean yet, either, have you?" That was Collum. "Come on."

We trooped back into the house and through the living room to the pool deck. I walked to the railing and stood there, mesmerized. Aquatic animals that defied description frolicked in the waves just offshore. A squawking seagull flew by, followed by a host of tiny, chittering birds.

"So I'm guessing new mammals are also being discovered?" I asked, as the guys joined me at the railing.

"How did you know?" Collum said. "And some have been brought back from extinction. There's an island off the coast that's populated now by actual dinosaurs."

"That has never ended well in the movies," I said, and paused. "I don't suppose any of those dinosaurs are purple, are they?"

"Not yet. But she probably got the idea for them from that song," said Collum.

"No doubt," I said. Then I turned to Conor. "*You* were extinct, more or less. Does all this" – I waved vaguely in the direction of the Pacific – "have anything to do with that?"

"Based on the timing, I think she tried it on me first," he said quietly.

Collum continued. "She wouldn't have had the power to do it on her own. But I'm sure she influenced the seed. I mean, while it was transforming so much else, why not?"

The front door opened. "Hello!" my mother called. Then she spotted us on the deck. "Raney! You're awake!"

"Could you guys, like, busy yourselves elsewhere?" I said to Collum and Conor. "I need to talk to her." I hooked a thumb toward Mam.

"Yes'm," Collum said, and escorted Conor through the door to my bedroom just before my mother stepped onto the deck.

"Hello, Mam," I said, and crossed the deck to hug her tightly.

"It's so good to see you up and around." She let me go, but held onto my shoulders with both hands. "You were asleep for ten…"

"Ten days, yeah, I know. The guys told me."

She glanced around. "Where did they get off to, anyway?"

Instead of answering, I said, "Have a seat."

"Uh-oh," she said. She perched on the edge of a chair while I rewrapped the blanket around me and plopped onto the chaise longue next to her.

I decided to get right to the point. "Why didn't you ever tell me you were still in love with my father?"

Her eyes dropped to her folded hands. Then she rallied. "It's not the sort of thing you discuss with your child," she said.

"It's not?" I said. "It's not germane for a child who's growing up in fear of her sperm donor to know that her mother has a soft spot for him?"

"It wasn't like that," she said.

"And how long have you known that my house is so close to his?"

"As soon as you told me you'd bought it," she said. "How could I not know? I knew exactly where his was, and I looked up yours on the map when you gave me the address."

"And you didn't *tell* me?" I shouted at her. "All these years I've worried about you. About your safety. About *hiding* you the way you hid me. And we just spent *weeks* chasing him across the world. *Weeks!* All the while I was worried about him finding you and… and *taking* you again. I couldn't let that happen! And then at the Door, when you were ready to sacrifice yourself, I thought it was *me* you were trying to protect. But it wasn't me, was it? It was…" I couldn't go on. Instead, I sank my face into my hands and sobbed. Nameless feelings tumbled through me. They were too much. It was all too much.

"Raney," Mam said. "My dearest daughter."

I felt her touch my arm. That was it. I threw off the blanket, the robe, and my pajamas, and dove into the pool.

A moment later, I heard another splash. *Get away from me!* I thought fiercely. *This is* my *pool! This is* my *sanctuary!*

But I didn't say it aloud, and she didn't leave. And gradually, the water did its work, and I was calm enough to hear her side of the story.

Mam had indeed hated my father, and she had absolutely tried to hide us both from him. That part was real.

Things changed after I bought the Malibu house. I'd sensed that Mam had avoided visiting me at first, but I didn't know why. Now it was obvious – she was afraid of running into Damien. Later, when she did finally come to see me, she made it a point to pass his place. She told herself she was conquering an old fear, but of course there was more to it than that.

And then one day, he saw her. All of her complicated feelings for him rushed back: love and hate, lust and fear. But losing her had tempered him, or so he claimed. He no longer wished to possess her – only to love her. Only to have her in his life again.

She gave him her terms and he accepted them. And to her surprise, he abided by them.

And then Surgat possessed him and everything changed. Of course the story he'd told me at Kalelea Heiau was bogus – Stone came looking for *him*, not the other way around. He'd followed my mother to my father's house, realized he had a perfect way to get back at me, and entered into the pact with Titania.

How the queen of faerie had gotten hold of the demon in the first place was an excellent question, but I had zero interest in tracking her down to ask her.

Anyway, all the rotten stuff that Damien had ever said to me, starting with his *come to meeeeee* routine at Lost Falls, had come from Surgat. And my father hadn't lied when he told me I wasn't Signor Buffon's target. As far as Damien knew, I wasn't. Stone had lied to *him*.

"Damien did say he wished we'd met under other circumstances," I said. We were still in pieces in the pool, conversing in a mind-link that came naturally to us.

"He still does," Mam said. "He'd like for you to be in his life, too. If it's too late for him to be a father to you, he'd like to be your friend."

I was quiet for a moment. "I need to think about it," I said.

"Of course," Mam said. "No pressure."

I laughed. "Right. Because you've never pressured me in your life."

"Maybe once or twice," she said. Then she laughed, too.

That afternoon, we had a party, and I was the guest of honor. Well, that's what I called it in my head. To everybody else it was a "going away and glad Raney's feeling better" party.

Niall and Kate Barth were flying home that night on a redeye out of LAX. "That's brutal," I said, remembering our flight in the other direction.

"It is," said Kate, "but then we'll be home. There are autumn chores awaiting us – putting the garden to bed for the winter – and getting ready for Samhain."

"It should be a little less spooky this year than it has in the past," Niall said, "what with that Key gone for good." The Elemental Keys had disappeared along with the Door.

"You think Dora will stop in for a visit, Da?" asked Conor.

"We'll let you know," he replied.

Gail had brought Ben Gelber along. They'd spent my convalescence together in the Elemental council's realm. Ben had spent his days – and many nights – studying all of the books in the council library that he could get his hands on. "What an amazing trove of information," he said. "I could live forever and never master it all."

Gail rolled her eyes, but fondly. She'd spent part of her time there negotiating with the council to let her go back to work for them. "They were impressed by the reports they received on my activities in the Otherworlds," she said. "Especially when they learned I'd rescued you."

So it turned out the seed's transformation caused quite a fireworks display. When it was over, Auntie Helen proclaimed that the team should fashion a new door and walk away. "And I said, 'Nothin' doin'. What if Raney's alive down there?' She said there was no way, and I said we at least ought to check. The guys sided with me, of course, especially Collum. But I finally just ignored her and went in after you."

"You disobeyed a direct order to save me," I said, "and your bosses are hiring you back anyway?"

She grinned. "Espionage allows for some creative leeway."

"So where do you go from here?" I asked. "Back to Harpers Ferry?"

She expelled a breath. "Yeah, for a little while. Ben and I are about ninety-five percent sure we're going to live in the council realm. But we need to settle our affairs here first. I've got to pack my stuff and put my house on the market." She looked at Conor. "I could sell it to you, but I hear you've still got one."

"I do. Collum never got around to cleaning it out." He grinned in his brother's direction. "If you're ever in the market for an estate administrator, hire somebody else. He's lousy at it."

"Hey, now, cut me some slack," Collum said. "We were kind of busy, and then we had to go out of town for a while."

"So you're going back to Harpers Ferry, too," I said. "And I guess Tiger's going with you." It made me sad to think of losing her, even though she'd been a giant a pain in the butt.

"Tiger is a free agent," he said. "She goes where she wants to go." He lowered his voice. "To be honest, I don't think she's forgiven me for not coming home to feed her after I died."

"Plus you hadn't scooped her box," I added.

Conor put the back of one hand to his forehead. "Oh, the humanity!" he quoted.

"She's always welcome here," I said. "But if she wants albacore, she's going to have to visit your mother."

What about shrimp?

"Depends on when I get a job," I said aloud.

Hmph. Maybe I'll live with Conor, after all.

"Suit yourself," Collum said.

Be sure to put in a permanent gate, though, since you're staying here.

"Now there's a surprise," Gail said, smiling archly.

Collum shrugged. "I've been in contact with the local land wights. They're moving back in everywhere, you know, now that the planet's been reset, and they think they can coexist with humans. But they're gonna need a go-between."

"And that's you," Gail said.

"Yep, that's me."

"Well, I think it's a splendid job for you," she said. "I really admired the way you managed Cloch at Lost Falls." Her snark was unmistakable.

"Hey, we worked things out eventually," he said with a grin.

Rufus and Annie were at the party, too, but they'd spent nearly all of it on a chaise longue next to the pool. Auntie Helen was inside, chatting with my mother and occasionally checking on the sad lovers on the deck. Finally she went to the door to the deck and yelled, "Hey, you two, get in here. We have some unfinished business to discuss."

We all took seats and looked expectantly at Auntie Helen. After a moment of silence, she began, "As you know, the Earth is governed by Nature, and Nature is a cycle. We have just renewed the Earth – but someday we will have to do it again. And once again, it will fall to the Elementals to do it."

"Swell," said Rufus. "What does that mean?"

"It means you four need to make new Keys."

"You're kidding," I said. "I have no idea how to make a Key."

"You didn't know how to renew the Earth two weeks ago," she said. "But you ended up doing a great job."

"I'm not sure that should be our metric," Collum said.

"Auntie," said Annie, "do we have to do this now? Like *right* now?"

"Well, no," said Auntie Helen.

"Good. Because I have something to say first." She turned to Rufus. "Marry me."

His eyes went wide. "We're doing this now?"

"Yes, we are. Right now." She propped her free hand on her hip; her other hand was trapped between Rufus and the loveseat. "I'm tired of waiting for you to ask, so I'm asking you myself."

"Well, okay. I mean, yes. Okay, yes." As the room erupted in cheers, he stood up, pulled her up after him, and kissed her thoroughly. Then he raised a fist in the air. "LET'S DO THIS!"

Of course I had to hug them both. "We'll send everyone an invitation when we figure out a date," Annie told me.

"We'll be there," I said. "Wouldn't miss it."

She lowered her voice. "You know, you could do the same thing."

I glanced between her and Collum, who was chatting with Rufus and looking at me. "Oh, I don't know. We haven't really discussed it."

"You should," said Annie.

"Thanks. I'll think about it," I said.

We all walked out the front door together. I'd intended to go along with the gang to the street while they waited for their Ubers, but my strength began to flag. So I leaned against the doorjamb and told everyone to go on without me. Collum gave me a quick kiss as he passed. "Be right back," he said.

"See you in a minute." I kissed him back, and waived gaily as they all departed.

As they went through the gate near the road, there was a bit of a commotion. Someone else – no, two someones – fought against the tide to come in. I straightened. One of them was Allen Owings from the Associated Press, and the other was...

"Sid?" I said in disbelief. Sure enough, it was my erstwhile agent – the guy who'd fired me by phone weeks before, while I was dodging the paparazzi in Harpers Ferry.

"Raney!" he cried, hurrying toward me with a broad smile. He grabbed my hand and pumped it up and down. "So good to see you up and around! Some redecorating scheme, huh?" He gestured vaguely at my yard. "I heard the whole thing was all your idea."

"Who did you hear that from?" I said. Then I glanced at his companion. "Never mind. I just figured it out. Hello, Allen."

He ducked his head. "I just came to thank you for letting me tag along on your journey," he said.

"You're welcome," I told him. If it had been my choice, I would have shut the fire portal in his face. But he didn't need to know that. Anyway, it was all over now.

"And I came to apologize," Sid went on. "This guy gave me the straight dope on what happened out there, and I know now that I never should have fired you. It was all a big misunderstanding." He wheeled his arms to indicate how big. "And I'm sorry. Truly, Raney."

"Thanks, Sid," I said. "I accept your apology."

He grinned. "Good, because we are back in business!"

"I'm sorry?"

He clapped Allen on the shoulder. "This guy here – this *magnificent* writer – told the story of your adventures in such enthralling detail that the studio wants to make a movie of it!"

Allen grinned sheepishly. "My boss says I might get a Peabody Award. Or even a Pulitzer."

"That's great," I said automatically, never tearing my focus away from Sid. "Say that again. The studio…"

"Wants to make a movie based on your story," he repeated. "Isn't that great?"

I was dancing inside, but fought to stay calm. "Maybe. How much are we talking?"

Sid named a figure, and my inner dancer went wild. "Who's the star?"

Sid laughed. "Well, *you*, of course, baby. It's your story."

My inner dancer rolled her eyes at *baby* but I beat back her retort. "Nope, not me. I'll be directing."

Sid blinked rapidly. "Well, you could do both," he said, in a tone that clearly said, *How the hell am I going to get the studio to agree to that?*

I crossed my arms. "Either I direct or there's no movie. And the rights are mine to sell."

"Of course! Of course! That'll all be in the contract." He side-eyed me. "But don't you want to be the star?"

I shook my head. "No thanks. I've had enough stardom to last me a lifetime," I said. "I'd rather get behind the camera. I think I might have a knack for directing."

He deflated a little. "I'll talk to the producers. It might be a hard sell."

"I have confidence in you," I said. Then a thought occurred to me. "Who's writing the script?"

Sid glanced at Allen, who ducked his head again. "Sid wants me to do it."

"He's a natural storyteller!"

"And I took a scriptwriting course in college." He smiled hopefully.

I sighed. Turning to Sid, I said, "We're not doing this if I can't direct. Got it?"

"Yeah, yeah, I got it," he said. "What's gotten into you, Raney? You used to go along with everything."

I gazed past him to my kaleidoscopic yard. "Motherhood," I said. "Motherhood's gotten into me."

When Sid and Allen left shortly thereafter, I realized I was exhausted. It had been a long day and I'd just gotten out of my sick bed that morning. All I wanted to do was get back in bed.

But it turned out I had one more tough conversation to go.

"So," Collum said as he settled in next to me, "Rufus got me thinking."

"You're going to switch Elements," I said.

He laughed. "No. How would I even...?"

"I dunno, but you should look into it. The way he slags a cell phone with his bare hands is kinda sexy."

"Raney." He stroked a lock of hair back from my face. "I love you."

I sighed. "I love you, too, and yes, I'll marry you."

His mouth dropped open. Then he began to laugh. "Was Annie working on you while Rufus was working on me?"

"Of course she was." I kissed him – a long, slow one that I would have followed up on immediately if I hadn't been so sleepy.

"Do I need to propose, then? Just to make it official and all."

"Nah," I said, snuggling into his chest. "We're good."

Author's Note

The first thing I need to do is thank you, my readers, for hanging in there. As you may know, I initially intended to push out this whole series in 2019. That would have meant publishing the book you're now reading in December. But deadlines got pushed back, and then in January I realized I needed to do a massive retooling of the whole series, including republishing the first three books before bringing this one out.

So here we are. And as we've been locked in our houses due to COVID-19, I've been editing and republishing a series that ends with a magical reset of the whole Earth, set to the tune of Barney's theme song. It's been a little surreal. But maybe it's for the best that the conclusion of Raney's story had to wait. In this crazy, chaotic time, I suspect we need a magical reset more than ever.

I had intended to write just these four books, but then Auntie Helen gave the team a new task. So there may be more *Elemental Keys* books eventually. Stay tuned to the blog – or you can join my mailing list by going to http://eepurl.com/xxw9d. Or, heck, do both.

As always, I have to thank my editor, Susan Strayer, for her eagle eye and her awesome advice. I could not have finished this project without her. And special thanks to members of my Woo-Woo Team for their excitement and encouragement for the whole *Elemental Keys* series. Feel free to join us at https://www.facebook.com/groups/WooWooTeam.

One last plug: Would you do me a favor, please, and leave a review? I'd appreciate it.

Take care of yourselves, okay? I want to see you all back here when this uncertain time is over.

Lynne Cantwell
April 2020

About the Author

Lynne Cantwell writes mostly urban fantasy and paranormal romance, with a dash of magic realism when she's feeling more serious. She is also a contributing author for Indies Unlimited. In a previous life, she was a broadcast journalist who worked at Mutual/NBC Radio News, CNN, and a bunch of other places you have probably never heard of. She has a master's degree in fiction writing from Johns Hopkins University. Currently, she lives near Washington, D.C.

Discover other titles by Lynne Cantwell:

The Elemental Keys
River Magic (original title: Rivers Run)
Bog Magic (original title: Treacherous Ground)
Gecko Magic (original title: Molten Trail)
Beach Magic

The Pipe Woman Chronicles Universe
Seized: Book One of the Pipe Woman Chronicles
Fissured: Book Two of the Pipe Woman Chronicles
Tapped: Book Three of the Pipe Woman Chronicles
Gravid: Book Four of the Pipe Woman Chronicles
Annealed: Book Five of the Pipe Woman Chronicles
The Pipe Woman Chronicles Omnibus

Where Were You When: A Land, Sea, Sky Anthology
Crosswind: Land, Sea, Sky Book 1
Undertow: Land, Sea, Sky Book 2
Scorched Earth: Land, Sea, Sky Book 3
The Land Sea Sky Trilogy

Dragon's Web: Book One of the Pipe Woman's Legacy
Firebird's Snare: Book Two of the Pipe Woman's Legacy
Spider's Lifeline: Book Three of the Pipe Woman's Legacy
Turtle's Weir: Book Four of the Pipe Woman's Legacy

A Billion Gods and Goddesses: The Mythology Behind *The Pipe Woman Chronicles*

The Transcendence Trilogy
Maggie in the Dark: Transcendence Book 1
Maggie on the Cusp: Transcendence Book 2
Maggie at Moonrise: Transcendence Book 3

Stand-Alone Novels
SwanSong
Seasons of the Fool

Short Story Collections
Back Home Again: The Five59 Stories, plus a few

Find Lynne on Teh Intarwebz:

Facebook: http://www.facebook.com/pages/Lynne-Cantwell
Twitter: http://twitter.com/lynnecantwell
Goodreads:
http://www.goodreads.com/author/show/696603.Lynne_Cantwell
Pinterest: http://pinterest.com/lynnecantwell
Ravelry: https://www.ravelry.com/people/lynnecm
Blog: http://www.hearth-myth.com

www.ingramcontent.com/pod-product-compliance
Lightning Source LLC
Chambersburg PA
CBHW050736230626
47052CB00002BA/352

* 9 7 8 1 7 3 4 7 7 7 9 1 8 *